SAVING
KRISTEN

SAVING KRISTEN

JACK WEYLAND

DESERET
BOOK

Salt Lake City, Utah

This is a work of fiction. Characters described in this book are the products of the author's imagination or are represented fictitiously.

Library of Congress Cataloging-in-Publication Data

Weyland, Jack, 1940–
  Saving Kristen / Jack Weyland.
    p.   cm.
  ISBN 1-59038-426-1 (pbk.)
  1. Mormon women—Fiction. 2. Stalking victims—Fiction. 3. Women college students—Fiction. 4. Police—California—Los Angeles—Fiction. 5. Los Angeles (Calif.)—Fiction. 6. Idaho—Fiction. I. Title.
  PS3573.E99S385 2005
  813'.54—dc22
                                        2004024179

Printed in the United States of America   21239
Edwards Brothers, Inc., Ann Arbor, MI

10   9   8   7   6   5   4   3

For Brian Kelly, Eleanor Knowles, Richard Peterson, Emily Watts, Richard Romney, and Duane Crowther.

As Jim Foote once observed, "Everyone needs an editor." That is especially true of me. I dedicate this book to my editors, who through the years have worked with me with such patience, kindness, and wisdom.

Thank you! I couldn't have done it without you.

CHAPTER ONE

Friday, June 12, 1998; Ashton, Idaho

Kristen Boone was born to dance, or at least that's what her mom and dad always said. They often talked about how even before she could walk, little Kristen would stand and sway back and forth to every song she heard.

Even though she had lived in tiny Ashton, Idaho, from the time she was six years old, her folks made sure she had the opportunity to have dance lessons.

And now, at fourteen, at her first youth conference, she stood on the sideline of the cultural hall and waited for a boy to ask her to dance.

If she had her choice, it would be David Carpenter, a boy two years older. Because David was best friends with Kristen's older brother, Zach, he was often at the Boones' house. David liked to tease her. She didn't mind, though, because he was never mean, and sometimes he would go out of his way to try to make her laugh.

She knew that David probably wouldn't ask her to dance because he was surrounded by girls his own age. Everyone liked David. Not only because he was good at sports, but also because he didn't exclude anyone from his circle of friends.

Growing up on a farm, David had learned to work hard. He was big-boned for his age and was already taller than most of his teachers. School and sports and work seemed to come easy for him.

Thomas, a boy her age, came up to Kristen. "So, you're at the dance, huh?"

She wondered how anyone could ask such a dumb question. "Yes, I am, Thomas. I'm at the dance."

Thomas wiped the sweat from his face. "I'm here too."

"I can see that, Thomas."

He was looking at his shoes. "We're both here at the dance."

"Yes, we are, but some of us are more here than others."

He seemed confused. He wiped his perspiring hands on his shirt.

"Would you dance with me?" he mumbled. "Just one dance, that's all. Please?"

She gave one desperate glance at David, hoping he'd rescue her, but he was having too much fun with the girl he was with. That was the trouble with David. He never seemed bored with people, like she was at that moment with Thomas.

She could hold out for someone better to ask her, but if she did she might never get to dance. She shrugged, frowned, and said, "Okay."

Once she began dancing, she forgot all about Thomas. She closed her eyes and pretended she was with David.

After the song ended, Thomas gave a sigh of relief. "Well, that's over. I promised my mom I'd dance at least one dance."

"Let's keep dancing."

He seemed surprised. "Why?"

"Think what you'll be able to tell your mom when you get home."

Thomas smiled. "Yeah. You know what? She said it wouldn't be so bad once I started. And she was right."

"Can we dance over by where David is?"

"David?"

"Yeah, David Carpenter." She nodded toward where David and his friends were gathered in a circle.

"Okay."

With each minute, Thomas became more animated. It was as if

Kristen had somehow made him think he was a good dancer. She didn't have the heart to tell him the truth.

Near the end of one song, Thomas was doing a chicken-strut kind of movement. As he threw his hand backward, he accidentally brushed the hair of the girl David was dancing with.

The girl turned around. "Excuse me? Do you mind?"

"Sorry."

She touched her hair in various places to see what damage had been done. "Maybe you shouldn't be out here with people who actually know how to dance."

"Sorry," Thomas said, looking at the floor.

"You know, you hit me."

"Sorry."

"He didn't mean anything by it, Mandy," David said. "Things like that happen. Are you okay?"

"I guess so, but look at my hair."

"It looks great. It always looks great." David said.

"I'm going to go see if I can fix it. I'll be back in a minute. Okay?"

"Okay," David said. "I'll wait for you right here."

Thomas looked devastated. David draped his arm over Thomas's shoulder and took him aside. "Hey, don't let it bother you. No harm was done."

"I'll never be any good at this."

"Oh, that's not true," David said. "Right before the accident, I was so impressed. You were doing way better than I did when I was your age."

"Really?"

"Oh, yeah. Absolutely. You're really coming along."

Thomas beamed at the compliment. "Thanks. You know what? I think I'll try another girl." He walked away.

David smiled at Kristen. "Looks like you've been abandoned. Want to dance?"

"Okay, I guess," she said, trying not to sound too excited, but her voice gave her true feelings away.

They began to dance.

"You don't have to do this, David," she said.

"Are you kidding? I'm the luckiest guy here." He looked around the cultural hall. "You're the best-looking girl here tonight. Look at you—blonde hair, blue eyes, a great dancer, good smile. A guy can't do any better than that."

"If that's true, then why do you call me Train Wreck?"

It was an old joke. Two years before, David had slept over at Zach's house. The next morning the two boys were watching cartoons on TV when Kristen came into the room. She was in her pajamas, and her hair looked like she'd slept in a wind tunnel. David had teasingly called her Train Wreck. The name had stuck.

"That was a long time ago. You look great tonight," he said.

It was a slow dance and without even thinking about it, she rested her head on David's chest. To her it felt like she'd come home.

"You baby-sitting tonight, David?" a girl teased.

Kristen, her face turning red, pulled away.

David smiled. "Hardly. This is Kristen. She's Zach's sister," he said.

"How cute. It's so nice of you to watch out for Zach's sister. You're always willing to do a friend a favor."

"This is no service project. Kristen and I are good friends."

"Still, I can't believe she was brave enough to ask you to dance," the girl said.

"I asked her. And I'm going to keep on dancing with her until the song ends."

"Whatever," the girl grumbled before walking away.

"You don't have to dance with me anymore," Kristen said.

"I'm happy to dance with you, Kristen."

"And it's okay if you want to call me Train Wreck."

"You know what? That wasn't very nice of me when I said that. From now on I'm calling you Kristen."

A short time later Thomas returned. "All the girls I asked to dance said they're getting ready to go home. So I'm back."

"Well, Kristen here is all ready for you," David said, backing away so Thomas could cut in.

David left to go look for Mandy.

Thomas gave her a toothy grin. "Don't worry. I washed the sweat off my hands."

Kristen's first reaction was to say something unkind to Thomas. But she didn't because she knew David never treated anyone like that. "It's okay, Thomas. Really."

After the dance, her brother, Zach, gave her a ride home. "What were you up to tonight with David?" he asked.

"Nothing."

"It must have been something. I was talking to some friends in the hall and a girl comes out and tells me you and David were dancing and you were draped all over him."

"We were just dancing."

"That's not what I heard. What is wrong with you anyway?"

"Nothing is wrong with me."

"From now on leave my friends alone."

She didn't say anything until they pulled into their driveway and then she slammed the car door on her way out. "David is my friend too," she said.

That night in her room, in her pajamas, she held a pillow and danced with it, trying to recapture the magic she had felt being close to David. As she rested her head on the pillow she was holding, she imagined David coming to the house to see her instead of Zach.

"David," she said softly to the pillow, "I know this will break your heart, but someday I'm going to leave Idaho. I'm going to be a famous dancer."

She tossed the pillow on the bed and danced out of her room and into the hall on her way to brush her teeth.

Saturday, June 13, 1998; Los Angeles, California

"Is this working?"

No answer.

"Oh, sorry, it wasn't turned on." As Commander Dutton pushed the power button, an ear-piercing, high-pitched tone brought pain to anyone sitting near the speakers.

Dutton turned the volume down and glanced over at Laura, his wife, who was trying not to laugh.

"Never turn a sound system over to a cop, right?" he joked.

A few people laughed.

"Look, I don't want to drag this out, but I want to thank everyone for coming to our first annual NORSAT picnic. I'd like to think of it as something we'll do every year from now on, but, of course, that will be up to Baker to decide when he comes back."

NORSAT, which stands for North Regional Surveillance and Apprehension Team, is a specialized unit of the Los Angeles County Sheriff's Department, created to investigate and arrest career criminal offenders. As commander of the unit, Dutton had nearly one hundred people working under him.

NORSAT's number was small compared to the nearly 10,000 working for the rest of the Sheriff's Department, but even so, they averaged over 500 career-criminal arrests per year with a 97 percent conviction rate.

Some of the men he worked with glared at him. Because of changes he'd tried to implement, many of them couldn't wait until P.J. Baker, the regular commander, would be back from finishing up his master's degree in criminal justice.

The family picnic had been Dutton's idea, but it never would have happened without Laura's help. Two weeks earlier, after work, he'd told her, "So far we've had only ten percent say they will come."

"What if you mail the invitations to the wives? And what if you promise there will be door prizes worth five hundred dollars?"

"Where do I get these door prizes?"

"Ask local merchants for donations."

"That's like blackmail. 'You kick in a prize or we won't watch your store.'"

"You are the most principled man I have ever met," she teased. "Why don't you let me work up the invitations to the wives?"

He was only too glad to have her do that. By asking around, Dutton also found a fund that would allow him to buy a few door prizes.

And so the picnic was a success. At least, attendance-wise.

"It's quite a sight to stand here and look at all of you with your families. Families are so important. I know mine is to me." He turned to Laura. "Do you all know my wife, Laura? I never could have pulled this off without her help. Let's give her a big hand."

Laura gave him a wait-until-we-get-home look, then smiled and waved at the smattering of applause. With her confident, casual manner, she was at ease in any situation. Much more so than Dutton, who was sweating from the tension he was feeling at that moment.

He paused. "I don't know if this is the right time to say this, but I'm going to do it anyway. Every morning before work I spend a few minutes thinking about my responsibility to make sure that every officer makes it home to his or her family at the end of the shift. I don't have to tell you, what we do is dangerous work. We deal with the worst elements of society at NORSAT."

The officers stared back at him, as if to say, "So, what else is new?" A few of them began gathering up their things, getting ready to leave.

"I've spent some time working up a program that I think will make everyone's job safer. But for it to work, I need everyone's cooperation. You wives, please encourage your husband to take the training and begin to apply it."

He paused, trying to decide if he should quit while he was ahead, or say more and risk alienating his men to an even greater degree.

"I have to be honest with you women. Not all the men at NORSAT have supported the changes we've tried to make in the way we do things on the job."

Every wife turned to her husband wanting to know where he stood on the matter.

"If I can just have a few more minutes of your time, I want to explain to you spouses what we have in mind."

The day before he had gone to a toy store and borrowed five wagons. One of them was red, the other four were green. He reached for the tongue of one of the wagons.

"Okay, suppose the red wagon here is really a car and in it are four hardened criminals with weapons. We have a warrant for their arrest. They're driving on a four-lane highway. We put an officer in an unmarked police car in front of them. He keeps far enough away so they're not paying any attention to him."

Dutton moved a green wagon in front of the red wagon, leaving about two wagon lengths between them.

"We also position one car on the right, one car on the left, and one in back." He positioned the wagons, leaving plenty of space between them and the red wagon.

"When we're ready to make the arrest, the front car slows down, the back car comes closer behind. One car pulls to the right and another to the left. And all the cars slow down until they come to a complete stop."

Dutton moved the green wagons in so they were touching the red wagon.

"Okay, so the bad guys are pinned in. They can't move backwards or forwards. The cars on the sides are so close the bad guys can't even open their doors. The officers who drove the cars in the front and on the sides jump out and run behind the car in the back. Okay, that's the situation. We call it containment."

Dutton knew all the officers didn't agree with him. He could tell that some of them were furious at him for going over their heads to get to their wives.

"Okay, what happens after this is critical. Any animal when it's trapped has a 'fight-or-flight' instinct. Bad guys are no different. If you give them a way out, they'll take it. But in this case they have no way to get out. We grab a bullhorn and say, 'You're completely surrounded. Escape is not possible. Just relax. We'll get back to you soon.' And then we wait for the fight-or-flight instinct to wear off.

"Nobody wants to die. These people have family, they have friends. They have attorneys who can maybe even get them off, or at least get them a reduced sentence."

One man most opposed to Dutton's changes stood up and grumbled to his wife, "Let's go."

She shook her head. "No. I want to hear what he has to say."

The officer, his face and neck red with anger, pointed his finger at Dutton. "You think you can buy us off with a few hamburgers? I can't wait for Baker to come back and put NORSAT back the way it used to be."

"Sorry you feel that way," Dutton said.

The man turned to his wife. "I said, let's go."

She shook her head. "I'm not going. And you know what else? I hope Dutton has this picnic every year, and if he does, I'm coming to it whether you do or not. If you don't change your attitude, you might be one of the ones who gets himself killed on duty. I'm not going to let you do that."

"Suit yourself. I'm going." He turned away, toward the parking lot.

Dutton cleared his throat. "Like I said, not everyone is in favor of this approach. After the fight-or-flight instinct has dissipated, which may take around half an hour, we ask them to throw out their weapons. When they have done that, we ask them to come out one at a time. If they do that, we promise them we will guarantee their safety. And we do. During the booking, and when they're in our jails, I want them as safe as if they were in their mom's home."

More grumbling was heard from officers who resented anyone urging leniency for criminals.

Dutton cleared his throat. "So, let me review. To do it right and to save lives, we need to have—" he put up a different finger as he ticked off each item—"containment, cool down, negotiation, and then arrest.

Shortcutting any one of those steps can result in shoot-outs that almost always end tragically."

Some of the officers were beginning to gather up their things and preparing to leave, but their wives were still listening to Dutton.

"I can see a day when we can go year after year without a shot being fired," he said, "with none of our officers being in the line of fire, with suspects turning over their weapons, with innocent bystanders being spared getting into the deadly crossfire that might wound or kill them. That's the vision I have for our department. And it can be a reality if we all pull together."

He ran his hand over his short-cropped hair. "Well, that's all I've got to say. I think there are some hamburgers and buns left, so if you're still hungry, help yourself. Also, you're welcome to take home the extra food. Once again, thank you all for coming." He reached down to the sound system. "How do you turn this thing off?"

Several wives came up and thanked him for trying to make their husbands' jobs safer.

As he was putting the PA system in the trunk of his car, four boys, all in their mid-teens, came up to him. They had their hands full of food and cans of soda pop.

"We got a question," the one in the lead said. He was a good-looking, blond, suntanned kid and was wearing expensive dark glasses. He was taller than the other boys and had a confident, easy-going manner. When he smiled, a dimple formed on his right cheek.

"What's your name?" Dutton asked.

"Chad Nieteri."

"Oh, sure, I know your dad well. He's a good cop."

Chad grinned.

Dutton turned to the others. "What about you guys? What are your names?"

Chad took the lead in introducing his friends. "This is Mike Collins and Tyler Felsted, and this is Andy Hazelton."

"Right. I know your dads. They're all good men."

"We want to be cops when we grow up," Chad said.

"Great! How old are you now?"

"Sixteen."

"Really? You look older. Well, if you do become cops, I'm sure you'll be as good as your dads. What's your question?"

"Once you arrest 'em, why did you say you wanted them kept safe? Wouldn't it be better to rough 'em up a little just to teach 'em that crime doesn't pay?" Chad asked.

"When cops beat up the people they arrest, then those people will eventually end up beating up cops. So if you want to make a cop's life safer, you treat the bad guys with respect."

"But if you beat 'em up bad enough, then maybe they won't do it again," Chad insisted.

"Cops just arrest people, they're not the judge and the jury. And they don't make people pay for their crimes."

Chad laughed. "What's the fun in that?"

Dutton frowned. "Well . . ."

"Relax, okay? I was just kidding," Chad said. "Thanks for the grub."

Dutton watched the boys saunter off, shadowboxing with each other.

"Trade me your Coke for my root beer," Chad said to Mike Collins.

"I don't want your root beer."

Chad playfully slugged Mike on the shoulder. "C'mon, it won't kill you to trade."

"Why should I? I got it first, so it's mine."

"Sure, fine," Chad said with a smile. He let Mike get ahead of him and then tackled him, grabbed his unopened can of Coke, and then helped him up. "Just kidding," he said with a smile. "Let's go."

"Hey, give my Coke back," Mike said.

"No, it's mine now. If you want it, you'll have to take it from me." Chad slipped the can into the pocket of his cargo pants and put up his fists. He tapped Mike on the cheek with his open hand. "C'mon, Mikey boy, show me what you got. C'mon, you chicken, I'm ready. Remember the last time you tried to take me on?"

Mike started to walk away.

Chad ran in front of him to confront him. "Oh, wait, I know! You want to show me how smart you are? You want to play chess again? How did that make you feel to be destroyed by me when it was my first game?"

Mike shrugged.

"Here, you can have my root beer," Chad said,

Mike shrugged and took the root beer Chad was offering him.

"Now everyone's happy," Chad said with a winning grin.

Dutton shook his head. He hoped that Chad, if he ever did become a cop, would never work for him.

He caught up with Laura, who was helping with cleanup. "Did we get rid of the extra food or are we going to be eating hamburgers for the next month?" he asked.

"We're good. There's a lot of potato salad left, but everything else is pretty much gone."

"Somebody in the world must like potato salad."

"Well, maybe so, but not in our family."

"So what do we do with it?" he asked.

"There's a ward potluck Thursday. If we refrigerate it, we could bring it for that."

"Great, as long as we reimburse the department for it."

"Captain Ethical Standards all the way, right?" Laura teased. "I'm sure you have the statistics on it, Officer Dutton. Please tell me how many law enforcement officers have started on their downward spiral into crime by not reimbursing their department for leftover potato salad. It must be in the thousands, right?"

"It's better to do things the right way."

She kissed him on the cheek. "I agree. You know I love the way you are."

That night after family prayer, Dutton took charge of getting the two older children to bed—three-year-old Adam, and Abigail who was eight. Gabe, their newborn, was already asleep. Adam was a little too young to concentrate on stories, but Abigail loved having him read to her. Her favorite stories were the ones with monsters and villains. She especially liked the way her dad's monsters roared.

Fifteen minutes later he joined Laura at the kitchen table where she was working on her Sunday School lesson. He wrapped his arms around her and kissed her in the crook of her neck.

"Oh, well, isn't that nice?" she said, hunching her shoulders and grinning.

He sat down and reached out for her hand. "Thanks for all your help on the picnic."

"It turned out okay, didn't it?"

"Thanks to you."

"Glad to help," she said, returning to her lesson.

"There's something else," he said.

"What?"

"That home evening lesson you gave Monday. It really helped me this week."

The previous Monday had been a hard day for Dutton and so in the beginning of Laura's family home evening lesson, he hadn't paid much attention. Then she asked him to read a passage from Alma 46 in the Book of Mormon.

"And it came to pass that [Moroni] rent his coat; and he took a piece thereof, and wrote upon it—In memory of our God, our religion, and freedom, and our peace, our wives, and our children—and he fastened it upon the end of a pole.

"And he fastened on his headplate, and his breastplate, and his shields, and girded on his armor about his loins; and he took the pole, which had on the end thereof his rent coat, (and he called it the title of liberty) and he bowed himself to the earth, and he prayed mightily unto his God for the blessings of liberty to rest upon his brethren, so long as there should a band of Christians remain to possess the land—

" . . . And when Moroni had said these words, he went forth among the people, waving the rent part of his garment in the air, that all might see the writing which he had written upon the rent part, and crying with a loud voice, saying:

"Behold, whosoever will maintain this title upon the land, let them come forth in the strength of the Lord, and enter into a covenant that they will maintain their rights, and their religion, that the Lord God may bless them."

Laura had asked Abigail a question. "What if Moroni had gone throughout the land, asking for people to help him defend their country, but nobody had volunteered. Would he have quit and gone home?"

"I don't know," Abigail said.

"Well, from the way he is described, do you think he was a quitter?"

"No."

"So what would he have done?"

"He'd have tried to do it anyway."

"Even if nobody would help?" Laura asked.

"Yes, he still would've," Abigail said.

That insight had encouraged Dutton to talk to the wives at the picnic about his plans to try to make his officers' work safer.

He opened the refrigerator and stared at the food inside, trying to decide if he should have a bedtime snack or not. "You want any potato salad?" he asked.

"No, I'm not that hungry." She smiled. "Actually, come to think of it, as far as potato salad goes, I'm never that hungry."

He closed the refrigerator and sat down again. "I want to be more like Captain Moroni at work."

She suppressed a smile. "You're not thinking of tearing up a perfectly good shirt and writing on it, are you?"

"Not that part."

"What part?"

"Doing what's right no matter what the consequences."

"You already do that, Dutton."

He was always amused when she called him by his last name. When they were first dating, she had asked him why at work he went by his last name.

He had looked around to make sure nobody was listening. "Don't tell anyone, but my first name is Kendall."

She could hardly keep from laughing. "Your secret is safe with me."

"I'm serious. If you're a Kendall at work, then before you know it, people start calling you Kenny."

"So?"

"A Kenny is someone you send out for donuts. That's not my style. I don't run errands for other cops."

Ten years later, married and with three kids, at work he was still Dutton.

He took a big bite out of an apple and returned to Laura. "When Baker comes back, he can change anything he wants, but I'm not going to just sit around and do nothing."

"You'll do a good job," Laura said. "You always do."

And he did. During the eight months that Dutton had been acting commander of NORSAT, the number of arrests where shots were fired had dropped dramatically.

When Baker finally returned, he worked six months and then took a job teaching criminology at Fresno State. Dutton was asked to continue as NORSAT commander.

CHAPTER TWO

Twenty-one-year-old Chad Nieteri was on his way to class at UCLA when he saw a girl walking toward him who caught his interest. Not just because of her looks, although that did intrigue him. She had long blond hair, blue eyes, and high cheekbones. Though she was carrying a heavy backpack, she walked with her head up high and had a kind of bounce to her step. But it was more than just her good posture or the way she moved. This girl made eye contact with everyone she met coming toward her, even smiling and saying hello to anyone who returned her gaze. This girl seemed glad just to be alive.

Chad stopped and turned away from her as she passed so she wouldn't notice him, waited a few seconds, and then began to follow her.

They ended up in a large classroom with elevated seating that was rapidly filling up with students. Chad found a seat one row above her and to her right. It gave him a good enough view for him to spot her name on a notebook—Kristen Boone.

During class, Chad ignored the lecture and used his laptop to go online and find out her class schedule, using a password he'd memorized while watching his adviser drop one of his classes for him. Chad noted that Kristen had two sophomore-level dance classes.

After class he lingered in the aisle so she'd pass by him on her way up the stairs.

"Excuse me, can I ask you a question?" he asked.

Smiling, she turned to look at him. That's when he saw how blue her eyes were.

"Were you here last time? I couldn't make it, so I need someone to let me copy their notes."

"Sure, no problem." Her smile was warm and friendly.

They walked together up the stairs of the classroom. "I think there's a copy machine somewhere in the building," he said.

"Yeah, there is."

"Oh, I'm sorry, do you have time? I don't want to hold you up if you've got a class."

"No, that's all right. My next class isn't until one."

Chad, of course, already knew that. "Thanks. I don't know anyone in the class and, well, I picked you because you seem like a really nice person."

She smiled again. "I try to be."

They started down the hall, looking for a copy machine. "Can I ask another question? Are you a dancer?"

She looked at him with a surprised expression. "How could you tell?"

"Just by the way you carry yourself. You're very graceful."

"Really? You could tell?"

"Absolutely. It shows."

They came to the copy machine, but there were two people ahead of them in line.

"By the way, I'm Chad Nieteri. And you're . . . ?"

"Kristen Boone."

"Where are you from?"

"Ashton, Idaho. How about you?"

"I'm from here."

"What's your major?"

"Law enforcement."

"Really? What made you decide on that?" she asked.

"My dad is a cop."

"So you want to follow in his footsteps?"

He smiled faintly. "Something like that."

It was their turn at the copy machine. Kristen flipped through the notebook and found her notes for the last class. "There are just two pages."

"The less for me to study then."

When they were done, Kristen put her notebook in her backpack. "Well, I guess I'll see you in class on Friday."

"Wait, let me at least show my appreciation. Can I buy you coffee?"

"Well, not coffee. Maybe hot chocolate though."

"Hot chocolate? This is California, okay? We don't drink hot chocolate."

"You're missing out."

"Okay, hot chocolate for you, but don't be surprised if I duck under the table if I see any of my friends. It'd be embarrassing for me to be seen with a girl who drinks hot chocolate in L.A."

"Do whatever you want," she teased. "I'll still be drinking my hot chocolate."

"You got something against coffee?"

"It's kind of a religious thing. I belong to The Church of Jesus Christ of Latter-day Saints. We're sometimes called Mormons."

"Oh, sure, I knew some Mormons in high school."

"Okay, so you probably know a few things about what we believe."

"Not really, but I'd like to learn."

"You would? Really? That'd be great."

"From you though, not the guys in the suits."

Chad wondered if he was being too obvious. A girl like her would not be won over just by his well-modulated voice, great tan, and his now curly blond hair. If she was like most Mormons he'd known, she would be looking for someone to convert. He could play that game. He'd be that for her until he got tired of her and moved on.

"Hey, I just thought of something. Why don't we drop by a Starbucks and order out their best hot chocolate, and then stop by my apartment and talk." As soon as he said it, he noticed a look of concern on her face.

"Actually, I need to go in a few minutes. I have a big test to study for."

At the student center cafeteria, they got in line. "Stand aside!" he yelled. "I'm with a girl who drinks hot chocolate!"

"And I'm with a slacker who never goes to class and bums notes off other students!" she countered.

They ended up at a table for two by a window overlooking campus.

"Well, how's the hot chocolate?" he teased.

"It's good. You want a taste?"

"No thanks. I'm afraid if I had even one sip, I'd have an uncontrollable urge to sing Christmas carols."

"Hot chocolate isn't just for Christmas."

"No, of course not. It's for ice skating, skiing, snowboarding, things we don't do much in SoCal."

He reached across the table and touched her hand with his forefinger. "Could we be serious for a minute? I need to ask you a question. When I asked you to go to my place, you got this weird look on your face. What was that all about?"

"Oh, well, it's just that . . . uh . . . I wouldn't feel comfortable being alone in an apartment with a guy."

"Someone told you how messy my place is, right?" he teased.

"Yeah, that's it. It's all over the campus. In fact, the headline in the student paper today is 'Nieteri Fails to Make His Bed for Fourteenth Day in a Row!'"

"Whoa, I'd better shape up then! Give me a day or two and it will be very clean."

"Actually, I'd still feel the same way."

"What? Are you worried about what kind of a guy I am?"

"Not really. It's just the way I was raised."

"I would never do anything you didn't feel comfortable with."

"I'm not saying you would. It's just my way of playing it safe."

He gazed out the window for a moment, then turned to look at her again. "You're right. You don't know that much about me. I can see why you wouldn't want to get yourself in a situation where things could happen. Maybe if we get to be friends, you'll see that I really am a good guy."

"I'm sure that could happen."

"Okay, one more question, and then we'll drop the subject. Have you taken some sort of a vow of chastity, or something?"

She blushed. "Well, yeah, actually, I have."

"Wow, that's even more unusual than the hot chocolate. I mean, around here anyway."

"There are lots of people who feel the same way."

He considered that for a moment. "You know what? If you think about it, that kind of a lifestyle makes good sense. Is it hard for you to make friends with a guy when you don't know what to expect?"

"Well, I do have to be careful."

"I can see that you would. Well, you can relax because I'm not someone you have to worry about, okay? But I would like to spend some time with you. Like we're doing now, for example. So, what do you say? Have we got a deal?"

"Deal." She stuck out her hand.

He looked strangely at her hand. "What are we doing here?"

"We're about to shake hands," she said.

"Really?"

She laughed, and it was the first time he'd seen her comfortable enough to let her guard down. He liked the way her eyes crinkled when she laughed.

They shook hands. "I've got to tell you something," Chad said. "I'm a little worried. What exactly does shaking hands mean in Idaho?" He gave her a suspicious look. "I haven't just bought a horse from you, have I?"

"Oh, no, not a horse," she teased.

"That's a relief."

"Just a pony."

"Really? I've always wanted a pony."

They talked for another hour and then she looked at her watch. "Hey, I've got to go to class."

"A dance class?"

"Yeah, it is."

"You suppose the teacher would let me come and watch?"

"I'm not sure I'd want you there."

"What if I went as a new member of the class?"

"Actually it's an all-girl class."

"What if I went as a girl?"

"I don't think you could get away with it."

"How come?"

"Too many muscles."

"You know what? You're probably right. Actually," he said with a voice so low he could hardly be heard, "I like to think of myself as a manly man."

She looked surprised. "Really?"

He pointed his finger at her. "You are in such trouble!"

She stood up. "Yeah, yeah. Well, I've got to go. Thanks for the hot chocolate . . . oh . . . and I did have fun talking to you. Oh, one other thing. The pony should arrive in a couple of days."

"He won't mind sleeping on a bunk bed, will he?"

"No, not at all. But if I were you, I wouldn't put him on a top bunk above you."

"Thanks. Let me walk you to class."

"Don't you have something else to do?"

He looked surprised. "Like what?"

"Oh, I don't know, go to class, study, take a test, write a paper, go to work."

"Not now, but I'll be busy tonight."

"Doing what?"

"Just a part-time job. Nothing too exciting, but it pays the bills. Let me ask you something. In class I noticed you were one of the few not using a laptop to take notes. How come?"

"Pen and paper are good enough for me."

"If you had a laptop, you'd use it though, right?" he asked.

"Yeah, probably. But I'm doing okay."

He walked her to class and stepped inside the room. It had wooden floors and mirrors on two of the walls. A couple of girls were already in their leotards and were warming up.

He spoke with a sing-song foreign accent. "Yah, I'm Lars, the new custodian. I'll be vashing the mirrors for the next hour. I hope dat von't bother anyone. Yust pretend I'm not here."

Kristen started laughing. "Get out of here and don't you go peeking in during class."

"Give me your number and I'll call you," he said.

"You got something to write on?"

"I'll remember it. Go ahead."

She gave him her phone number.

He started down the hall, then turned around and said, "I'll call you tonight, okay?"

"Okay."

*   *   *

That night Chad got together with Mike Collins, Tyler Felsted, and Andy Hazelton. In fourth grade, at the beginning of the school year, they'd spend part of their lunch hour outdoors, climbing in a tree. One day a teacher found them and called out, "You monkeys need to come down from that tree now. Recess is over." After that, the four of them always called themselves the Monkey Boys.

At that time in their lives they all wanted to follow in the footsteps of their dads, but as they grew up, each of them found reasons to pull away from his family, and they became disillusioned with law enforcement as a career.

22

In recent months they had begun meeting in bars where they would huddle at a small table in the corner and drink and talk. Sometimes, like tonight, they finalized plans.

"Okay, just like last time," Chad said. "Tyler, you'll go in with me."

Tyler nodded. He never talked much. In some ways he didn't need to. Standing six-feet-four and weighing well over two hundred pounds, he had what it took to enforce the mean streak he'd had even as a kid.

Andy was slight of build and not very smart. Chad didn't have much confidence in him. Just like when they were kids, Andy spent most of his free time playing video games. "Andy, you'll be our lookout."

"I can do that."

Mike had been Chad's best friend all the way through school. He was still someone Chad could depend on. "Mike, I want you around back, in case anyone tries to make a run for it."

"All right, and then you'll let me in after you're inside, right?"

"Yeah, like last time."

At ten-thirty, Chad stepped outside to call Kristen. When she answered, he said, "Do you like marshmallows with your hot chocolate?"

"Chad, I'm glad you called. I was just thinking about you."

"Hey, I've been thinking about you all night. That was fun, being with you today. It's refreshing to find someone who has values and standards. Your beliefs are really interesting. And guess what? My roommate had a copy of the Book of Mormon. So I dusted it off, and I'm going to start reading it, soon as I finish a few other projects."

"Chad! That is so cool. If you have any questions, we can talk about it."

"Great. Well, look, I don't want to keep you. I just wanted you to know that I've been thinking about you."

"That is sweet of you to call."

"Did you just say the word *sweet*?"

"Sorry."

"No. It's all right. Is that the way everyone talks in Idaho?"

She laughed. "No, just in Ashton. It's not like the rest of the world.

We don't even lock our doors at night. That's been a hard thing for me to learn here."

"I've got to see this place. Maybe I'll come visit you sometime."

"That'd be great."

His friends came out of the bar. Mike pointed to his watch as a reminder for Chad to get off the phone.

"Well, I've got to get some sleep so I'll stay awake in my classes tomorrow," Chad said. "I'll talk to you later."

He turned off his cell phone.

"Who was that?" Mike asked.

"Just a girl."

"You going to tell us about her?" Tyler asked.

"Later. Let's go to work."

They drove to a commercial storage facility where a few months earlier, they had rented two units. They stored a leased car in one of them. The second unit looked like it should be in a police station. Police equipment: authentic badges, bulletproof vests, weapons, raid jackets identical to those used by the L.A. police department, official L.A. police baseball caps, smoke grenades, handcuffs, crow bars, surveillance cameras, two-way radios, and ski masks were stacked on some gray metal shelving.

Twenty minutes later, they drove out of the facility dressed as cops, each wearing a weapon in a holster, a raid jacket, and a police department baseball cap.

Thirty minutes later, after circling the block a few times, they pulled up in front of a run-down house. From his place in the passenger seat, Chad asked, "Well, what do you think?"

"Let's do it," Mike said.

"Okay, you guys. Remember, we're professionals," Chad said.

Mike disappeared into the darkness around the side of the house. Andy remained in the car to be the lookout.

Chad drew his weapon, and Tyler carried a heavy, steel battering ram. They crept up onto the darkened porch, and Chad nodded. Tyler used the battering ram to shatter the lock and blast the door open. Chad threw in a smoke grenade and yelled. "Police! Throw down your weapons!"

Two startled men looked up from the couch where they had been seated, watching television. One of them immediately leapt up and ran out of the room, toward the back of the house. A second later, they heard Mike's voice. "Hold it right there. I've got you covered. Get back inside!"

Mike pushed the frightened man into the room and tripped him from behind, sending him sprawling forward onto the floor and then cuffed his hands behind his back.

The man on the couch put his hands up, cowering against the back of the couch. Chad approached him, dragged him by the hair off the couch and onto the floor, and handcuffed him. As he read the man his rights, he looked at Tyler with a slight grin. "You have the right to remain silent . . ."

Chad shoved his gun into the man's cheek. "Where's the money?"

"What money? What's going on?"

Chad grabbed him by the hair again and wrenched his head upward. "We're not playing games, punk. Where's the money?"

"It's in the floor under the couch," the man grunted.

Chad and Tyler each grabbed one of the man's arms, lifted him up, and shoved him onto a chair. Chad glanced at Tyler. "Get the money."

Tyler pulled the couch out and looked at the floor. "I don't see anything."

"Get down on your knees and feel around," Chad said. He turned to the man on the couch. "What else you got?"

"Nothing. This is a money house. We don't sell."

"We're going to do a complete search of the place. If you're lying to me, I'll make sure you spend the rest of your life locked up."

"I got it!" Tyler called out, pulling a black garbage bag out of a hole cut in the floor. He opened the bag.

"It's full of money," he said.

"This is all the evidence we need," Chad said.

Tyler stuffed the money into a heavy canvas police evidence bag.

Chad activated the radio on his collar. "Report in."

"All clear," Andy said.

"We're going now," Chad said, speaking to the two men. "We're sending a patrol car to pick you up and take you to the station. If either of you has moved when they come, I'll tell them to shoot you for resisting arrest." He knelt down and pressed the muzzle of his gun against the neck of the man on the floor. "You understand me, punk, or do I have to blow your head off?"

"I understand."

"Good." He stood up and motioned to his friends, "Let's go."

They hurried to the car, got in, and drove away.

As they sped off, Chad opened the bag. "Another operation well done, men. Let's go back to headquarters and fill out our reports."

Tyler laughed. "It kills me when you talk like that, Chad."

"We're professionals. Just like our dads, right? Except they're all idiots."

They returned the car to their storage unit, stripped off their police gear, and then left.

At Chad's apartment, they counted the money. One hundred and fifty thousand dollars.

"So how much is that for each of us?" Andy asked.

Chad looked at him and shook his head. "You ever hear of something called arithmetic?"

"I never was very good at math."

"Don't worry, I'll take care of it. Okay, first of all, we've got expenses."

"Like what?"

"We need to buy more cars."

"What for?"

"Just in case we have to leave town in a hurry. We need four cars in storage units around the city, and they have to be cars that we don't normally drive, just some junkers that we can afford to use and then abandon when we're through with them. And we need a 'drop-off' house, a rental place we can go after we've ripped off a dealer. We can't keep coming here to my apartment. We've got to keep things separate. I'll take care of that too."

Chad counted out ten thousand dollars. "This will get us started on that.

"Also, we need to pay off our cop friends who keep us posted. I'm suggesting we take ten thousand off the top for every job and use that money as a kind of investment into the business."

Chad set aside another ten thousand dollars.

"Plus, we always need to be upgrading our communications equipment. I mean, after all, we are professionals, and we need to keep current with what our brothers in the force are using these days. Let's go with another ten thousand for that." Chad counted it out.

Chad divided the remaining money equally into four piles.

"Andy, we're each getting thirty thousand dollars. Not bad for a couple hours of work, right?" He stepped back. "Take the pile of your choice, boys."

They each grabbed a pile and stuffed it into their pockets.

"Don't spend it all in one place," Chad said. "Don't flash it around. Don't tell anyone about tonight. Mike, you don't say a thing to Summer. And Tyler, you don't say a word to whoever it is you're seeing now. And, Andy—oh, I forgot, you're not seeing anyone, are you? Don't say anything to your mommy, okay?"

He looked at each of his grinning friends. "Now, let's go have a few drinks and celebrate," Chad said. "We deserve it. Good work, men."

"Tell us you're proud of us and how we've made the town a little safer," Tyler said cynically.

They returned to the bar where they'd been earlier and started drinking again.

"So, tell us about this girl of yours," Mike said.

"She's from Idaho. She's a Mormon."

"What does that mean?"

He smiled. "It means I'll be her first guy."

"And when is that going to happen?"

"Can't say for now. When she's ready."

"Aren't you the guy who still holds the record for consecutive nights in your apartment with a girl you met the same day? So, what's the deal?"

"There's no challenge in that for me anymore. Give me a girl with high moral standards . . ." He paused, then added with a grin, "Someone to corrupt."

"Sounds interesting. Let us know how it goes," Mike said.

"And for sure, let us see the video afterwards," Tyler said.

Chad laughed. "Maybe I will, but maybe not. This one is different. Maybe I'll save the video just for me."

"You never have before," Tyler said with a big smile.

"Okay, you win. I'll show the video if you guys will help me win her trust."

They continued drinking until two in the morning.

*   *   *

When Kristen Boone left her home in Ashton, Idaho, to attend UCLA, she did so without her parents' full blessing. Her mom was okay with the idea, but her dad wasn't at all sure.

During high school Kristen had gotten heavily involved in dance and drama. She had always enjoyed dancing, but she had never thought of herself as an actor. Then in her junior year, at the urging of the school choir director, she tried out for the school play and won a secondary role. She did well in the one scene where she had a solo, and that was when she began thinking she might like to make a career of acting. Her decision to go to UCLA was influenced a lot by the fact that it was located near Hollywood. In her dreams she imagined herself somehow being discovered by a big movie producer.

In her senior year Kristen won the lead in the school play. They had done *Man of La Mancha*, and she had really enjoyed the experience. The rehearsals were long and demanding, and she often got discouraged, especially in the beginning when she was trying to learn her lines, the music, and the dance routines. But after she got into it, she loved it. And on opening night, when the audience stood and applauded her performance, it was a thrill like nothing she had ever experienced. She was also amazed by the reaction of the kids at school. In the weeks following the show, they looked at her like they never had before. The boys paid more attention to her, and she especially enjoyed seeing the envy in some of the popular girls' eyes. For the first time in her life she felt as though she was really somebody.

Her dad wasn't enthused about her leaving home to go away to college, especially not to California. In a weak moment, when Kristen and her brother, Zach, were young, he had agreed to take his family to Disneyland and had never gotten over the trauma of driving the freeways. Rulon Boone had lived his whole life in Ashton, and he had a healthy mistrust of the big city and especially what he liked to call "show business types." It was not an easy thing for him to agree to let his little girl go off to pursue the kind of dreams she had about becoming a movie star.

Kristen's mother had what Kristen saw as a more enlightened view of things. She was the one who had always seen to it that Kristen took dance and piano lessons. And seeing her daughter on the stage in the role of Dulcinea had been a thrill for her too.

It had taken some convincing to get her dad to agree.

"Daddy, I don't see what the worry is," Kristen had argued. "It's not like I'm going to go down there and throw away everything I've been taught."

"I'm not saying that," Rulon answered. "But things are . . . different in California. I just don't feel right about it. Why not just go down to Rexburg to BYU–Idaho? If you want to live on campus, I'll pay for it. But at least you could come home on weekends."

"They don't have the kind of program I'm looking for," Kristen argued.

She didn't dare say that she had grown weary of tiny Ashton and the kids she had grown up with. So many of them had no idea about what was fashionable in clothes or music or anything. She was anxious to break away from the farm and experience the excitement she had come to feel was missing in her life. That was why she was grateful to have her mother take her side.

"Rulon, honey," her mother had said, "you don't need to worry about Kristen. You know how she's been raised. They've got an institute at UCLA, and she'll have a ward to attend and a bishop to look after her. Besides, the exposure to other people and the kind of education she'll get there will be invaluable."

In the end, he was outvoted. But that didn't mean he had to be happy about it.

*   *   *

On Friday, Chad waited for Kristen outside her class. He held a tall cup of hot chocolate with whipped cream on the top.

"There you go," he said, handing her the cup. "Starbucks' finest."

"Chad, that is so nice. Thank you."

"I've got something else for you too."

"What is it?"

"It's a surprise. Let's go sit down."

They went outside the building to a bench on the lawn under the trees. Once they sat down, he made her close her eyes. He pulled a laptop out of his book bag. "Okay, open your eyes."

She looked at the laptop and then at him. "I don't understand."

"This is your new laptop." He opened it up and turned it on. "It's got all the latest features."

"I don't know what to say."

"That's easy. Just say, 'Thanks, Chad.'"

She shook her head. "Chad, no, it's too expensive."

"Not really. I got a good deal."

"I don't want you to spend your hard-earned money on me."

"I was at the store buying a few things. It was on sale, and I thought you'd like it, so I got it."

"That's really nice of you . . . but I can't accept it."

"Why not?"

"I just don't feel right about it."

"Why's that?"

She avoided looking at him. "I don't want to hurt your feelings, but . . . it feels like you're trying to buy my friendship."

He looked hurt. "What can I say? I'm a generous guy. Ask any of my friends, they'll all tell you the same thing. I'm always giving them things."

"Chad, I can't accept this. I'm sorry."

He slipped the laptop back into his backpack. "No problem. I'll take it back. It was just a whim anyway. Bad idea, I guess. Don't worry about it."

"I'm sorry," she said. "Thanks for understanding."

"It's no biggie. Oh, by the way, after class I want to take you on a drive. I got a new car."

"So, Big Spender, who died and made you rich?" she teased.

"Actually, my grandfather left me some money. I got the check in the mail yesterday."

"I am so sorry," she said, the smile on her face turning into a grimace. "I was just joking. I didn't know your grandfather had died."

"It's okay. It happened a year ago. I'm over the shock. It's taken the lawyers that long to get it to me."

"Are you saving any of it for school?" she asked.

"Oh, yeah, sure."

After class, she rode with him in his new car—a brand-new convertible with leather seats and a polished, wooden dashboard.

"It's a beautiful car, Chad."

"I could bore you with a lot of details, but let me tell you, it's fast. Lots of horsepower."

"Do you like to drive fast?" she asked.

He shook his head. "Not all that much. But I know I'll have to know how when I'm finally on the force." He laughed. "I know it sounds strange, but I can't wait to get out there and start catching the bad guys. Kind of weird, right?"

"No, not at all. I think it's great—that you're so focused."

He turned into an apartment parking lot. "This is where I live." He parked the car. "I know you don't want us to be alone in my apartment, but could you just do me a favor? I'll open the door, and you can peek in, and then we'll go. I really went to a lot of work cleaning it up, and, well, if you could just take a look, then all my work won't be for nothing."

"Chad, I know you'll think I'm strange, but . . . I'm not comfortable—"

"C'mon, there's nothing to worry about. I just want to show you that I'm not a slob."

"So we'll just be there a minute, right?"

"I promise."

"Well, okay."

When they reached his apartment on the third floor, he opened the door, and with great flair, announced, "Ladies and gentlemen, may I present Chad's apartment!"

He stepped aside as she looked in. Every surface gleamed. Nothing was out of place.

"Chad, it looks great."

"Thanks. It took me quite a while, but you know what? Now that it's in good shape, I think it will be easier to keep clean."

"I'm sure that's true."

"Oh, there's one other thing I thought of while we were driving over here. This might take me a few minutes, so if you want to come in and sit down, go ahead. Whatever you want. I'll be in my room." With that, he left her at the door.

After a few minutes of standing in the doorway, she went inside and entered the kitchen. "I'm doing an inspection of your kitchen, Chad," she called out.

"I hope I pass."

"Well, don't expect any favors." She opened the oven. "Wow, what a surprise."

"What?"

"The oven is spotless. Did you clean it?"

"Oh, yeah. I was there for hours, slaving away with a mop and bucket."

"A mop and a bucket?"

"Maybe not, huh? How about a rag? Yeah, I remember now. It was a rag and a bucket. No water though."

"Somehow I'm not sure I believe that."

"The truth is I've never actually used the stove."

"That makes more sense," she said.

"Oh, I almost forgot. There are some fresh vegetables and dip in the refrigerator, if you're interested," he said.

"Okay, thanks."

Fifteen minutes later, he called out, "Sorry, this is taking so long. Give me five more minutes."

"What are you doing?"

"I can't tell you. It's a surprise."

A few minutes later he returned carrying a laptop. "This is my old laptop. It's pretty old and doesn't have what I need now. So on our way over here, I decided to keep the new one. But I really don't need this anymore. I could just throw it away, but if you can use it, it's yours. If you can't, I'll just toss it in the dumpster on our way out."

"Chad . . ."

"What? Do you want it or not? It's up to you."

"Well, there's no reason to just throw it away. I'm sure I'd use it if you gave it to me."

He handed her the laptop. "I cleared out all my old files. That's what took so long."

"I can't believe you'd do this for me."

"Are we going to shake hands again?" he asked.

"No, not at all." She stepped close to him and gave him a hug with her one free arm. "Thanks, Chad. This is so generous of you."

"No problem." He moved away from her. "Hey, I know you don't feel comfortable here, just the two of us, so let's go."

"Sorry to be so paranoid," she said as they walked to the car.

"Hey, it's no big deal."

"Don't get me anything else, okay?" she told him.

"Fine, but I can still feed you, right?"

She smiled. "Anytime you want."

"Great. Three of my friends want to meet you. We've been best friends since fourth grade. We're going out to eat tomorrow at a famous restaurant in Malibu called Granita. You want to come along?"

"Will I be the only girl?"

"No, of course not, they're all bringing someone. We were thinking of leaving here about two in the afternoon. We'll probably do a little shopping, maybe walk along the beach, and eat around six. I'll have you home by, say, ten-thirty. How does that sound?"

"It sounds great."

"Good. I'm glad you can make it."

CHAPTER THREE

The next day, a Saturday, Chad knocked on Kristen's door promptly at two o'clock. When she opened the door, Chad was standing there, wearing shades, a loose-fitting, white linen shirt, tan shorts, and sandals.

Kristen was wearing Keds, jeans, and a freshly ironed, short-sleeved yellow blouse.

"I wasn't sure what to wear," she said. "Is this place really fancy?" She glanced at his shorts and sandals.

"You're just right," Chad assured her. "Nobody really dresses up in California. You can wear just about anything you like. You ready to go?"

"I am." She grabbed a backpack. "Chad, look at me, I'm locking the door. Isn't that so Californian of me?"

"Oh, yeah," Chad said. "For a minute there, I thought you were a native."

Two cars were parked at the curb. One was Chad's convertible with the top down. A couple was sitting in the backseat. Chad introduced Kristen to them first. "Kristen, this is my boy Tyler and his friend Asia."

Tyler grinned and tossed his head, and Asia gave a wave. She was wearing shorts and a halter top and was tanned to the extreme. Her bleached hair was done up in corn rows.

Chad took Kristen by the arm and led her to the car parked behind his. The windows were down, and a rap song was playing on the stereo. They had to lean down to look inside the low car. Chad shouted above the music, "These useless guys are Mike and Andy. And their friends, Summer and Calli."

The girl he called "Calli" corrected him. "It's Halle," she said. Leaning forward from the backseat, she hollered at Kristen, "And what's your name?"

"I'm Kristen," Kristen shouted, giving a wave to the four in the car.

They drove in two cars along the Pacific Coast Highway. Chad took the lead, with the other car following.

The sun was shining in a clear, blue sky, and it was unseasonably warm for January. "This is so beautiful!" Kristen said, looking at the beach and ocean.

"Haven't you ever come out here?" Asia asked.

"No, not really. I've pretty much stayed on campus."

"We've got to show her how gorgeous California is, so she'll never want to go back to Idaho," Chad said. "All they've got there is snow and hot chocolate."

When they got to Malibu, Chad said, "This is such a great day! It'd be a shame to waste it. What do you guys think about going swimming?"

"I didn't bring a suit," Kristen said.

"Me, either," Asia added.

"That's no problem. We can buy suits and towels at one of the shops." He turned to Kristen. "What do you think? You want to swim in the best surf in California?"

"They have great shops in Malibu!" Asia said. "Very expensive, of course, but since going swimming is Chad's idea, he'll pay for everything. Right, Chad?"

Chad looked back at Asia in his rearview mirror and flashed her a big smile. "Yeah, sure, it's on me."

"That's what I love to hear," Asia said.

Chad used his cell phone to let Tyler and Andy and their dates know about their change in plans.

They found an exclusive store in Malibu with a wide variety of swimming suits. Chad and his friends just went to the rack, chose a size, and were done in five minutes.

The girls took more time because they had to try the suits on in a changing room.

Ten minutes later three of the girls had picked out suits, but Kristen was still in the changing room as a store clerk brought one suit after another to her.

"What's keeping her?" Chad asked Asia.

"She can't find anything she likes."

"I'll go talk to her," Chad said. He went to the curtain leading into the changing rooms. "Kristen?"

"Yes?"

"Is anything wrong?"

"I'm sorry. It's just . . . I can't find anything I'm comfortable wearing," she said softly.

He lowered his voice too. "I understand. Well, if it's any consolation, nobody will notice what you're wearing because everybody dresses this way in California."

"I know, but I wouldn't feel right wearing a two-piece suit. Even the one-piece suits aren't very modest."

"Okay, look, I don't want you to do anything you feel uncomfortable about. We don't have to go swimming, okay? It was a dumb idea anyway."

"But everyone else wants to go, don't they?"

"Yeah, but so what? There are lots of things we can do today besides swimming."

Kristen didn't immediately respond.

"Anything wrong?" he asked.

"I was just thinking. We've only just met, and you're being so good to me."

"Hey, what can I say? I just want you to be happy, that's all."

Kristen let out a big sigh. "Thank you."

"Wait a minute. I just thought of something. What if you get a suit and then wear a T-shirt over it? That way you can be as modest as you want."

She paused. "That might work."

"Great. Pick out a suit and put it on, and I'll go find you a T-shirt. We'll just dump our clothes in the car and go straight to the beach from here."

They went swimming. Kristen loved the waves and the beach. The T-shirt Chad picked out for her was wet and heavy in the water, but it did its job in helping her feel modest. Unlike the other girls who just got wet and then lay down to work on their tans, she waded out into the surf and enjoyed trying to ride the waves. She wasn't very good at it and was pummeled a few times when the waves plunged down on her. She came up sputtering, her swimming suit full of sand and her eyes full of salt water.

Chad and his friends were all strong swimmers. She was amazed at how they knew just when to start swimming to catch a wave and then ride it toward shore, just their heads and shoulders sticking out of the water as they were swept along.

After a time, she pulled herself out of the surf, her legs feeling weak, and her ears full of water. Chad and Mike caught a wave and followed her to shore. They waded out of the water, and Chad said to her, "Mike and I need to talk to you. Let's take a walk." They stopped where the girls were sunbathing, and Chad handed Kristen a towel so she could dry off. Then he led her away from the girls who were totally into sunning themselves.

"Go ahead, Mike," Chad said.

"Have you ever heard of Antonio Fellini?" Mike asked.

"Not really."

"What do you expect? She's from Idaho," Chad teased.

"Okay, have you heard of the movie *One Life to Waste*?" Mike asked.

"No."

"How about *Ambrosia*?"

"Sorry."

"If it's not Disney, she hasn't seen it, so just tell her," Chad said, grinning.

"Antonio Fellini is a big movie producer," Mike said. "And he's my uncle. Okay, I don't see much of him because he's gone a lot, but we e-mail now and then. Anyway, I happen to know he's looking for someone to play the female lead in his next movie. From what he's told me, I think you'd be perfect. So I was wondering if you'd mind if I took a few pictures of you. I'll e-mail them to him, and we'll see what he says."

Kristen thought about her secret dream of being discovered by some big-time producer. But she had always pictured that happening in a restaurant or the lobby of some hotel, not on a beach with her hair all stringy and wet and wearing an oversized, sopping wet T-shirt. "I'm not an actor. I'm a dancer," Kristen said.

"Well, that's not a problem," Mike said. "You've got a pretty face, and you carry yourself well. That's basically all he needs. He likes to work with unknowns."

"That's because he doesn't have to pay them much, right?" Chad joked.

"Well, that's part of it. But I think the real reason is he likes the freshness that untrained actors bring," Mike said.

"What kind of a movie is this going to be?" Kristen asked.

"Something you'd be proud to have your name on. Antonio Fellini is first class all the way. He already has two Academy Awards. If he likes what he sees, it could be an opening into the business. It's a chance thousands of women in this town are looking for. What do you say?"

"This could be a really good opportunity for you," Chad said.

"I don't know what to say," Kristen said.

"Just one thing, it would be better if the other girls didn't know about this," Mike said confidentially. "Especially Summer. She might not like me promoting your career. She's a real beauty, of course, but she's not what my uncle is looking for, and I really don't want to have to explain that to her. I'm sure you understand."

"All right. I'll keep it to myself," Kristen said.

"Let's move a ways off and we'll take some pictures. We'd better hurry because it's about time for us to go to the restaurant."

They walked along the beach to a cove where they wouldn't be seen by Summer and the others.

"Okay, so we're just going to take a few pictures," Mike said. "Oh, one thing. My uncle will want to see *you*, not some mammoth-size L.A. Lakers T-shirt."

Kristen hesitated and then removed the T-shirt. She was chilled and had goose bumps all over.

"That's much better," Mike said.

Mike gave her directions of what to do for each pose. A few minutes later they were done. "Very nice. Give me a minute to edit these and then I'll send 'em to my uncle."

"You did really well," Chad said to Kristen, wrapping the towel around her shoulders.

"This is so unexpected," she said.

"That's the way things go sometimes," Chad assured her. "You know what?" He pointed at the huge houses on the bluff above the beach. "In a year, you could have your own house in Malibu."

"Okay, I've sent the pictures to my uncle," Mike said. "He's in Italy now finishing up a movie, but, depending on his schedule, we might hear from him even tonight."

They changed out of their swimming suits in a beach-side, public shower building with cold, wet sand on the cement floor. One of the toilets in the girls' side was stopped up, and the place smelled rank. Kristen couldn't believe how casual the other girls were about changing. It was like it was no big deal. They just took their swimming suits off right out in the open and put on their clothes. Kristen at least tried to turn her back to them.

As they were changing, Tyler's girlfriend, Asia, glanced over at Kristen. "So, where'd you get your underwear, girl? JC Penney's?"

The two other girls laughed.

Kristen blushed. "I don't know for sure. My mom got it for me."

"My mom used to shop for me too," one of the girls said, " . . . when I was in first grade."

A little after six, as they entered the restaurant, Kristen was overwhelmed with the lavish interior of Granita, the famous sea-god fantasy-theme restaurant in Malibu.

"Oh, my gosh, we're going to eat here? It must be very expensive."

"Well, a little, but we only come here a couple of times a year, so enjoy the experience," Chad said.

As they were being shown to their table, Kristen couldn't get over the decor. "It's like being under water," she said.

"Yeah, it is," Chad said.

"Let's start with some champagne," Mike said to the waiter before they ordered. "This could be a very special day for Kristen, a day she'll remember for the rest of her life."

"Why's that?" Summer asked.

"Just being here with you guys," Kristen quickly said. "Thank you very much for a great day."

A few minutes later the waiter went around the table pouring champagne into each of their glasses.

"None for me, thanks," Kristen said.

"But I got it for you," Mike complained. "This is a time to celebrate and be happy."

"Back off, okay?" Chad told Mike. "Kristen doesn't drink."

"Why not?" Asia asked.

"It's a part of her religion," Chad said. "And I totally support her in that."

"Well, it would've been nice to know that before I ordered," Mike said. "I got this especially for you. I thought you'd want to celebrate."

"I'm sorry," Kristen said.

Mike looked at her, then shook his head. "You try to help someone out, and what thanks do you get? Kristen, do you have any idea how much champagne costs at a place like this?"

"I said back off, Mike," Chad said. "She doesn't drink. It's part of her religion. As her friends, I think we should honor the way she's chosen to live her life."

Mike thought about it and then said, "Well, okay. But, Kristen, why don't you humor me by just taking a taste. Just one taste. One taste won't kill you, will it?"

Chad had his arm around Kristen's chair. He whispered in her ear. "I think Mike's right. Just take one taste and this will all blow over. Besides, Mike ordered it just for you."

Kristen had never violated the Word of Wisdom, but she didn't want to offend Mike. Besides, it didn't look so dangerous—just like sparkling white grape juice. So she took a small taste of the champagne.

"That's my girl," Chad said with a big smile. "Now let's quit arguing and just have a good time."

At first Kristen felt guilty for drinking, but after a few sips it didn't seem like such a big deal. By the time their main course came, she had finished the glass of champagne. Chad immediately poured her another glass.

Everything about the experience was new and exciting to Kristen. Even the waiter explaining the specials of the day delighted her. "Sautéed Maine lobster with mango vinaigrette and shaved pepper salad."

"That is so beautiful," Kristen said. "Could you go through that again just for me?"

"Why don't you let me order for you, Kristen?" Chad asked.

"That would be good."

The conversation during dinner was lively and fun. Halle turned out to be quite a mimic, and she entertained them with her impersonations of politicians. The guys were all witty, and even though Kristen didn't understand their inside jokes, she felt very happy and grateful to be with such beautiful people.

After a spectacular dessert, they wandered along the shops and art galleries that lined the streets in Malibu. Under the influence of the champagne, they decided to pretend to be foreign tourists as they shopped. They each tried to speak English with an accent. The only problem was that Mike's accent kept slipping from one country to another. He'd start talking in a German accent to a shop clerk and end up within a couple of minutes speaking with an Irish brogue. Kristen, with Chad at her side, stood nearby and laughed until her stomach muscles ached.

"Looks to me that the champagne is doing its job," Chad said.

"Is that what it is?" Kristen said with a smile. "Well, whatever it is, I like the way I feel."

They drove down the coast and ended up on the pier at Santa Monica. As they passed a tattoo parlor, Summer said, "Hey! Let's all get a tattoo. Something to remember the day by?"

"I'm up for that!" Andy said.

They entered the shop. "Let's find a pattern we can all agree on, and we'll get identical tattoos," Summer said.

"How about an American eagle on our arms?" Tyler said.

"How about a butterfly?" Asia said.

"I am not getting a butterfly!" Andy declared.

"Okay, what if everyone picks what they want, and then Chad pays?" Asia asked.

"Now you're talking," Halle said.

Kristen held back while the others made their choices.

"Do you know what you want yet?" Asia asked Kristen a few minutes later.

"I'm not sure I even want one," Kristen said.

"Why's that?"

"Well, for one thing, my folks would kill me if they found out."

Halle smiled. "Put it where nobody will see it. That's what I'm going to do."

Kristen still wasn't sure. She wondered if it would hurt. It was hard to imagine doing something so permanent to her body, even if it was small and hidden.

There was only one tattoo artist in the shop, and so it soon became apparent the process was going to take a long time.

"You want to wait in the car with me?" Chad asked.

"Okay," she said.

They sat in the car and talked. "You look like you're having a good time," he said.

"This has been a great day. Your friends are so much fun. The people I grew up with are nothing like this."

"I'm glad it's been a good day," he said.

They kissed a few times. Kristen wasn't worried at all about Chad anymore. In fact, she wasn't worried about anything.

After a while, Halle came out of the tattoo parlor. She was walking gingerly and seemed to be in pain. "He's ready for you now, Kristen."

Kristen nodded and stepped out of the car. She noticed she didn't seem to have full control of her muscles.

A few minutes later the tattoo artist closed a curtain around his work area. Kristen stood next to the table.

"You want yours in the same place as the girl before you?" he asked.

"Where was that?" she asked.

"On the buttocks."

She hesitated.

"Get up on the table, lying face down. Oh, and you'll need to get rid of some of that clothing."

Kristen hesitated. "Really?"

"I can't put tattoos through clothes, okay? I've got to see some skin. Just hurry up, I've got people waiting."

"I . . . uh . . ."

"What?"

"I can't do this. Sorry." She pushed the curtain aside and walked out of the shop.

"That was fast," Halle said when she stepped outside onto the sidewalk.

"I decided not to do it," she said quietly.

"Well, you're better off. I'm not going to be able to sit down for a week."

At ten o'clock Chad insisted that they leave even though not everyone had gotten their tattoo yet.

Back in L.A., Chad and Mike dropped Summer off first and then headed to Kristen's apartment.

Mike, in the backseat, checked his cell phone. "Kristen!"

"What?"

"I just got an e-mail from my uncle. Listen to this! 'Got your pictures. The girl looks good. Will arrange screen test after I get back.' That means you're in!" Mike said. "My uncle wouldn't want to do a screen test with you unless he felt like you're what he's looking for."

"When is your uncle coming back from Italy?" Kristen asked.

"I'm not sure, but certainly sometime in the next month."

"I can't believe it! This is so exciting!" Kristen said, shaking her head.

After they arrived at Kristen's apartment, Chad walked her to the door. "Hey, thanks for coming with us."

"I'm the one who should be thanking you."

"You know what makes me happy?" Chad asked. "How well you fit in with my friends. They all like you. Maybe we can all get together again someday soon."

"I'd like that very much. Oh, and thank you for the swimming suit and the T-shirt, and the dinner and taking me swimming, and everything."

"Hey, you're welcome. You know what? I'd really like to go to church with you sometime. Is that allowed?"

"Church?" she asked.

"Yeah. That's not a problem, is it?"

"Well, no, I mean, I guess not."

"I've got some things I need to get done tonight, but if I'm not up too late, I might be able to make it tomorrow. What time do you want me to come by for you?"

"You really want to go to church with me?" she asked.

"Why not? I shared my life with you. Now it's time for you to share your life with me."

"Well, church starts at nine, so if you could come by around eight-thirty, that would give us plenty of time to get there."

"I'll see how things go," he said. "At any rate, I'll call you in the morning, maybe around seven-thirty and let you know. Is that okay?"

"That would be really good. There's just one thing."

"What's that?" he asked.

"I shouldn't have had anything to drink tonight, so I feel a little guilty."

"Oh, I bet there're lots of Mormons who drink. Is it really that big of a deal? I mean, you didn't get drunk or anything."

She sighed but didn't say anything.

"Well, I'd better go. See you tomorrow." He leaned over and kissed her and then bounded down the stairs.

After he left, Kristen couldn't stop feeling guilty about drinking the champagne, but after thinking about it, she decided that Chad and Mike were right, it hadn't killed her. Besides, it was all turning out for the best. Chad was going to church with her in the morning.

She also couldn't stop thinking about the possibility that she could be in a movie directed by . . . she couldn't remember his name, but she knew that he was famous. She tried to imagine what it would be like to be rich and popular.

Instead of reading the scriptures as she usually did before she went to bed, she turned on the TV and watched a movie. She tried to pay attention to the way the female lead played her part. *I have so much to learn if I'm going to be a movie star,* she thought. But something else kept running through her mind. She couldn't quit thinking about her dad and what she had said to him: *Daddy, I don't see what the worry is. It's not like I'm going to go down there and throw away everything I've been taught.*

At two-thirty in the morning, she finally turned off the TV. Usually, before slipping between the sheets, she always knelt by her bed and prayed. But she didn't feel much like praying, so she just climbed into bed and a short time later fell asleep.

CHAPTER FOUR

That night, just after midnight, the Monkey Boys raided another drug house. When they broke down the door, there were three men in the house.

One of them pulled a pistol and took a shot at Chad but missed. Reflexively, Chad fired back and wounded the man.

Tyler slammed one of the men in the face with his fist, knocking him unconscious.

The third man pulled a knife and confronted Chad, but hearing the shots, Mike had come in through the back of the house. He stepped quietly up behind the knife-wielding man and clubbed him on the back of the head with the butt of his pistol, dropping him to the floor.

Panicked at the noise and violence, the three of them hurriedly ransacked the house until they found the stash of money and then they ran outside.

Andy drove up to the curb. They jumped into the car and took off.

"This never should have happened!" Chad raged. "Somebody messed up! Why were there three tonight? There's always been two before."

"How could we know there'd be three?" Mike asked.

"We need surveillance! We need to have round-the-clock surveillance before we do a job. We need to get organized!"

He looked down and swore. "Look at this! My pants and jacket are covered with blood. And it's on our shoes, so that means it's in the car.

It's everywhere. If it takes all night, we've got to get rid of any and all evidence that would link us to this."

"Where do you want me to go?" Andy asked.

"Did anyone see us?"

"I don't think so," Andy said.

Chad began shouting. "You don't think so? What do you do while we're inside getting shot at? If you can't do the job, just say so and I'll get someone who can."

"I don't think anyone noticed us," Andy said. "The shots weren't that loud."

"Did you notice anyone opening their bedroom windows and looking out?" Chad asked.

"No," Andy said.

"You don't know for sure, though, do you? What were you doing, playing another one of your stupid video games?"

"When I heard shots, I went back to the car and drove it in front of the place. I figured that's what you'd want me to do."

A minute later Andy took a turn too tight and too fast.

"You're driving too fast!" Chad yelled. "Slow down, you idiot! You want to get us picked up? You think a cop might wonder why I've got blood all over me?"

"I thought we were in a hurry," Andy said.

"You know what the trouble with you is? You think too much. From now on let me do the thinking."

They'd all seen Chad like this before and knew the best thing was just to be quiet.

"I thought you were going to rent a drop-off house," Tyler finally said.

"I'm working on it, okay? And while we're at it, why do I have to be the one who does everything? Why can't you guys pull your weight?"

"We will," Mike said. "Just tell us what you want us to do."

"Right now our first priority is to get cleaned up," Chad said. "We'll go to my place and wash our clothes and shoes in the bathtub. And then in the morning we'll go to a car wash and clean up the car."

"If someone did spot us, they might have called the cops and given them our license number," Mike said. "So maybe we should switch cars."

Chad folded his arms, rested his head on the back of the front seat of the car, and sighed. "All right, let's do that. We don't need to panic. Let's go back to where our cars are parked."

Nobody said another word until they pulled up to their storage shed. They drove the car into one of the units and closed the door.

"I think we should split up," Mike said. "If the cops are on to us, they'll be looking for four guys. We can all wash our clothes in our own apartments." He put his hand on Chad's shoulder. "Don't worry. If anyone saw us leave the place, we look like cops, so to them, it's just another example of police brutality. It's going to be okay."

Chad sighed. "All right. Let's split up the money and then separate."

Half an hour later they went their separate ways.

At one-thirty that night, Chad was in his bathroom, kneeling over the bathtub, scrubbing his blood-spattered raid jacket, pants, and shoes.

He desperately wanted to get some sleep, but his mind was still racing. He had never intended to shoot anyone, and he was shaken by the sudden violence of what had happened. He still had to worry about the car they'd driven. He filled a bucket with water and drove to the storage shed and washed the floor mats and then the seats.

It took him until three o'clock to clean up the car.

Now I can go home and get some sleep, he thought. But as he stepped out of the car, he noticed a faint trail of blood from someone's shoes.

He took the water still in the bucket and a rag he'd used to clean the car and got down on his hands and knees and scrubbed the floor of the storage shed.

Even after that, he realized he had used the same water over and over to wash and to rinse, so that most likely what he had done was to spread a thin solution of blood all over the shed.

He drove to a park and filled the bucket with clean water and returned and redid the floor.

By four-thirty he was so exhausted he crawled into the backseat of the car and fell asleep.

He might have slept most of the day, but a little after eight he heard a father and his son at a nearby storage unit talking as they hooked up a boat trailer to their car.

He sat up and looked at his watch. He remembered his promise to call Kristen.

"Hello," she said a moment later.

He tried to sound wide awake. "Good morning, Sunshine! How are you doing today?"

"Great. I had such a good time yesterday and last night. Thank you so much."

"I'm glad you enjoyed it. Look, I really had planned on going to church with you this morning, but I got called out for work, and so I won't be able to make it. I definitely plan on going next week though."

"What time is it?" she asked.

"A little after eight."

"Oh, wow, is it that late? I must have slept in."

"It probably won't hurt if you miss church one Sunday, right?" he asked.

She hesitated, then said, "If I hurry I can probably still make it. But is there anything I can do for you?"

"I don't think so, but thanks for asking. Oh, there might be one thing. Do you have a car?"

"I do. I don't drive it much because I'm trying to save money."

"I have some clothes I need to donate to the Salvation Army tomorrow. They're just some old things I've outgrown. I'll be busy most of the day. If I bring them by your place later this afternoon, do you think you could drop them off in the morning on your way to school?"

"Oh, sure, I could do that."

"It would be great if you could."

"After all you did for me last night, I'd be happy to do that for you."

"That's one thing about you I really appreciate. I can always count on you to help someone in need."

Back in his apartment, the last thing Chad did before he went to sleep was phone his friends and tell them to bring the clothes they'd worn the night before so he could give them to Kristen to drop off on Monday.

She's going to turn out to be very useful to me, he thought with a smile. *In so many ways.*

*　　*　　*

Kristen hung up the phone and sat up on the bed and tried to decide what to do. Jonathan, a friend of hers from institute class, had left her a voice mail the night before, offering to pick her up for church and asking her to call if that wouldn't work out. He would be there in less than half an hour. She'd just woken up, and with her hair a mess, there was no way she could get ready that fast.

She knew Jonathan would be willing to wait for her, but that wasn't the only problem. She had a headache and a strange taste in her mouth. She brought her hand up to her mouth and breathed out, trying to find out if her breath smelled of alcohol. She couldn't tell for sure.

"I can't ever do this again," she said to herself. She paused. "Especially on a Saturday night."

She reached up and touched her head, got up slowly, and padded into the bathroom. She took a couple of aspirin and then stood there looking at herself in the mirror.

I don't look any different, she thought. *Nobody will be able to tell what I did last night. I should go to church. I could skip taking a shower and not eat and not spend much time on my hair and still be ready when Jonathan comes.*

A minute later, she went to her closet to pick out a dress to wear to church. Just looking at her Sunday dresses made her feel guilty. *I can't go to church, not after drinking last night. I'd feel too guilty. People would know something was wrong. I can't go this week. I'll go next week, though, for sure.*

She wrote a note for Jonathan, telling him she was sick and wouldn't be able to go, taped it on the outside of the door, and then crawled into bed and went back to sleep.

When she woke up at two that afternoon, she decided that, even though she hadn't gone to church, she could redeem herself by doing the reading for her institute class.

First she decided to eat something and see if there was anything to watch on cable. While fixing herself a bowl of cereal, she found a program where a popular, up-and-coming Hollywood actress was being interviewed about her work. The woman was impossibly pretty, with perfect teeth, flawless skin, beautiful hair, and a gorgeous outfit. She was seated comfortably in a large chair in a beautifully furnished room.

Kristen had never paid much attention to movie stars before, but with the prospect of her being in a movie, she found the interview interesting. She wondered how old the actress was and how she had been able to develop the self-confidence she obviously had.

"You've never done a nude scene in any of your past movies," the interviewer asked. "Why's that?"

"I just don't think it's necessary. Most nude scenes in movies are not an integral part of the story. They're usually just thrown in."

"What if someone gave you a script where a nude scene was vital to the story?"

"It would depend on what kind of a movie it was."

"I'm talking about a serious film, with a reputable director. For instance, a movie like *Titanic*."

"Well, then, I'd have to consider it. I think that, as an actress, one must always be true to one's sense of artistic integrity."

Kristen thought about that, then slowly nodded her head.

She glanced at her institute manual. With her head still aching, she couldn't work up any enthusiasm for doing her reading. She finished her cereal, put her bowl and spoon in the sink, clicked off the TV, then lay down on the couch. Her mind went back to the night before and how much fun it had been to be with Chad and his friends. She thought about how exciting it had been when they had kissed and how relaxed and happy she had felt under the influence of the alcohol. These were her thoughts as she drifted off to sleep again.

*   *   *

For Elder David Carpenter, who was serving in a small branch in upper New York state, seven-thirty Sunday morning meant that he and his companion, Elder Salazar, needed to attend the branch's priesthood executive committee meeting. Because the branch didn't have a mission leader, President Edwards, the branch president, had asked David and his companion to meet with them each week.

Most of the time he and his companion sat there with very little input to the meeting. But on that Sunday, they seemed to be the main reason for the meeting.

"It has come to my attention that you have been teaching a family by the name of . . . Rizzuto," President Edwards said.

"That's right, President," David said. "We've talked about them in this meeting for the last few weeks."

"That may be so, but this week I found out that the father's name is Billy Rizzuto. Is that correct?"

"Yes, President."

"Do you know that Billy Rizzuto has a criminal record? Do you know he served time in the state penitentiary? Do you know any of that? And if you do know it, why have you not mentioned it to us in this meeting?"

"We didn't know about it until this week. When we interviewed him and his family for baptism, he told us about his past."

President Edwards's voice grew louder. "You've interviewed him for baptism without asking me how I feel about having a convicted criminal in our branch?"

"President, he's thirty-seven years old. It's true that he held up a liquor store when he was eighteen. He served five years in prison for that. When he was released, he got a job in construction, and a year later married a wonderful woman. They now have five kids."

"I was living here when he held up the store, and I know the woman who was working at the store when he held it up. He pointed a gun at that poor woman. It terrified her. She couldn't sleep for months after that. Let me ask you a question. What if she decides to come to church? What's she going to say when she sees him here? I really don't think it's right to bring convicted criminals into our branch."

"You are the one who presides in this branch, President, and I certainly respect the way you feel," David said. "But I wonder if my companion and I could talk with you privately sometime today."

"We can talk all you want, but it's not going to change my mind."

"We'd like to meet with you anyway, if that would be okay with you."

"All right, let's get together after the block."

Just before church, David and Elder Salazar waited in the foyer for the Rizzuto family to show up.

"What will we do if President Edwards says we can't baptize the Rizzutos?"

"I'm sure we can work it out," David said.

"But what if we can't? You know, we don't need his permission to baptize converts."

"I know that, but it's always better to work with branch and ward leaders," David said.

"Edwards can be a very stubborn man. Like the time he wouldn't let us baptize on a Sunday."

"Things will work out. I'm not worried," David said.

"Maybe you aren't, but I am. I haven't had a convert baptism in four months, and if this doesn't work out, well, then I've had it with Edwards. You can keep meeting with him Sunday mornings, but I'll stay in the hall."

"Things have a way of working out," David said.

The Rizzutos didn't show up until five minutes after sacrament meeting had started. They seemed like an ideal family. Their kids were excited to see the elders.

The elders and the Rizzutos sat in the overflow area. After the meeting, a few people came up to welcome the family, but not as many as before when the elders had someone to church. Neither President Edwards nor his counselors went out of their way to greet the family.

After the block of meetings was over, when they sat down in President Edwards's office, David asked if they might have a prayer.

President Edwards asked Elder Salazar to say the prayer.

After the prayer, President Edwards turned to David. "Go ahead, Elder. It's your meeting."

For David, feeling the influence of the Holy Ghost was like being in a very pleasant room where it was quiet and where time seemed to slow down. It was a place where he felt at peace. And that is how he felt at the moment.

David never talked about it on his mission, but he had been tutored by the best when he was growing up. Not only by his dad, a man he loved and admired, but also by a number of General Authorities.

His dad had been called to be stake president when David was just starting junior high school. From then on, every year when a General Authority came to preside at a conference, he would stay in their home. After the Saturday night meetings, the family and the visiting authority would have dessert in the living room and talk. Those had been some extraordinary occasions.

Each of the Brethren was different, and yet they all paid attention to David and his brothers and sisters, asking each one about their lives, and encouraging the boys to prepare for their missions.

At those times these men would often teach and bear testimony. And for David it was like receiving personal instruction to him from Heavenly Father about how to live his life.

On his mission, David had never told anyone about these

experiences. He kept them to himself, but he held sacred the counsel he had received from each General Authority.

As they talked with President Edwards, David felt the Spirit. He believed that all he had to do was be prayerful and express his feelings, and Heavenly Father would do the rest.

At the same time, he understood the importance of honoring President Edwards in his position of branch president. There could be no animosity between them.

David didn't feel that it was his job to do a high-pressure sales pitch. It was simply to let the Spirit do whatever persuading needed to be done.

"You're here to try to talk me out of preventing a convicted felon from being baptized, so go ahead," President Edwards said.

"That's not why we're meeting, President Edwards," David said.

"Why are we here then?"

"To try to come to an agreement about what Heavenly Father wants."

President Edwards paused. "For you it's the same thing, isn't it, Elder?"

"Not always. Have you always been a member, President Edwards?" David asked.

"No. I joined after my wife and I were married."

"What happened to cause you to want to be baptized?"

"After our first son was born, my wife, who was already a member, decided to go back to church. I didn't go with her, but . . ." he paused.

"What?" David asked.

"She seemed very happy whenever she came home from church."

"Did she talk to you about what it was like for her at church?" David asked.

"No, not at first. She didn't say much of anything about it."

"What made you decide to look into the Church?"

President Edwards, lost in thought, stared at a painting of the Savior on the wall. "Angie became more loving to me and to our family. That was it. No lectures, no preaching, just kindness. At first I thought she was doing it to get me to change my mind about the church. But after a few months I realized that wasn't it. How she treated me didn't depend on whether I took the missionary lessons or not. The simple fact is that going to church had made her a more loving person."

"That is an amazing testimony about the power of love," Elder Salazar said.

"Yes, it is." He sighed. "It truly is."

"So what happened once you figured that out?" David asked.

"When I told my wife I would like to start attending church, she nearly fell off her chair. From then on, we went as a family. And then after a while I started to take the missionary lessons in our home. A month later, I was baptized."

"Where do you suppose this love that your wife found at church comes from?" David asked.

President Edwards smiled and shook his head. "I see where you are going with this, Elder. It comes when we realize that God is our Father and that Jesus is our Savior and Redeemer. Once we feel through the Spirit that they love us, then our lives are never the same again."

"That is where it comes from, isn't it?" David said.

President Edwards smiled. "And you're trying to get me to say that Billy Rizzuto has felt the same love that my wife and I experienced. Is that it?"

"I believe he has, President."

President Edwards sighed. "Then I guess we don't have much more to say. I'll trust you elders to let me know when you think he's ready for baptism."

"We're shooting for three weeks, President."

"Three weeks? Well, all right then, we'll do whatever we need to do to get ready for that day."

They stood up and shook hands and parted.

"That was awesome!" Elder Salazar said as they left the church.

"You are never to brag about this, Elder. We didn't do anything, do you understand me? It wasn't us. It was Heavenly Father, it was the Spirit, but it wasn't us. If you go bragging about spiritual experiences like they are your personal victories, then Heavenly Father might be reluctant to give you more experiences like that."

"Okay, sorry."

"The most important thing we can do out here is listen to the Spirit."

That night as he got ready for bed, David had a thought run through his head that he should write to Kristen Boone.

It doesn't make sense for me to write her, he thought. *Her brother, yes, but not her. I don't even know where she is.*

On Monday, the thought persisted, so after writing his folks, he wrote to Kristen and put the letter in its own envelope and asked his mom to forward it to her.

Dear Kristen,

I'm not sure why, but I've been thinking about you lately.

Zach and I have written each other a couple of times. Sounds like he's doing really good in Ecuador. I'm doing good too.

We're working with an amazing family now. When the father was young, he made some serious mistakes and ended up going to prison. But now he is a good husband and father, and he looks forward to being baptized with his family.

I know that God is willing to forgive us of our sins. It has been such a great experience for me to work with this family. I know now more than ever before that we can be forgiven when we mess up. All we have to do is make changes in our life and then put our trust in Heavenly Father and the Savior.

I am grateful to Father in Heaven for his great plan of happiness. And I am grateful for the atonement of Jesus Christ. I have a strong testimony of the restoration of the priesthood to the earth.

Write me sometime, Train Wreck. I'd like to know how you're doing. Also, could you send me a picture?

Sincerely, your brother in the gospel,
Elder David Carpenter

*　　*　　*

A few days later, late at night, Chad walked Kristen to the door of her apartment.

She stumbled on one of the stairs.

"You okay?" he asked.

"I'm fine."

"How many beers did you have?" he asked.

"Just one," she said.

He laughed. "Really? Just one? I would have guessed two or three."

"No, it was just one."

"Did you have fun tonight?" he asked.

"I did, Chad. I always have fun with you and your friends."

"What was the best part of the night?"

"Getting to drive the boat."

He smiled. "I kind of thought you enjoyed that. You know what my first clue was? When you wouldn't let Asia do it."

Kristen gave him a mischievous grin. "I was there first."

They kissed a few times and then he whispered in her ear. "Would you like to invite me in?"

She pulled away. "Not really."

"That's okay. I'm a patient man. Are you going to church tomorrow?"

She felt a wave of guilt pass over her. "I can't decide."

He shrugged. "Whatever you want. Well, I'd better be going." He kissed her again and then left.

After he drove away, she got her mail. She was surprised to find a letter from David Carpenter.

She read the letter a few times, feeling more guilty each time. Finally, just before starting an R-rated movie Mike had recommended to help her learn how to be an actress, she threw the letter in the garbage.

CHAPTER FIVE

"Good morning. Can I talk to you?" Dutton said to Delilah Thatcher, his secretary, as he entered the office shortly before eight o'clock.

She followed him into his office. "What's on your mind, Chief?" She always had a sarcastic smirk on her face when she called him chief.

"Friday is Law Enforcement Day at my daughter Abigail's school. I told 'em I'd come. How about helping me figure out what I can bring that would be a hit with the kids."

"Okay. I'll get back to you after lunch. What else?"

"What have I got going today?"

"Henderson called. He'll call back this afternoon."

"What's it about?" he asked.

"He didn't say."

"I'm going over to the jail to visit Robert Armstrong."

"Who's he?"

"He's an officer, but not one of ours. He worked as a deputy at the San Dimas Station. He's a young guy and, actually, didn't work there very long. He just got convicted of manslaughter for accidentally shooting a pregnant woman during an unauthorized drug raid."

"Unauthorized drug raid? What does that mean?"

"It means the guy was out of control."

"Why are you visiting him?"

"The commander of the San Dimas Station called and asked me to look in on him. They're keeping him in the county jail instead of sending him to the state pen. He's pretty depressed, and they're afraid he'll try to commit suicide."

Delilah went to her desk and brought back a package of dark chocolate. "You'd better take this with you then. Chocolate always makes me feel better. I bet it will do the same with Armstrong."

An hour and a half later Dutton sat down with Robert Armstrong in a private visiting area in the county jail. "My name is Dutton. I'm the commander of the NORSAT unit with the Los Angeles County Sheriff's Department. I've been asked to check in on you and see how things are going. I've asked for you to be made a trustee. That should make your life a little easier."

"Thanks." Armstrong sighed. "Even with what happened, I still feel like I'm a deputy sheriff."

"I understand."

"This whole thing was just a mistake in judgment."

"It happens in police work." Dutton handed him the package of chocolate.

"What's this for?" Armstrong asked.

"My secretary suggested it. She says chocolate always makes her feel better."

"Thanks." Armstrong opened the package and put a piece of chocolate in his mouth. "This jailhouse grub gets pretty old," he said.

"If you don't mind me asking, how did you get yourself in this mess?" Dutton asked.

"Why should I tell you?"

"No reason. I was just curious, that's all."

Armstrong shook his head. "What a mess to be in."

"Yeah, I know. I don't envy you one bit."

They talked for a few more minutes, and then Armstrong quietly said, "I guess I'll tell you. Maybe it'll help someone."

"Maybe so."

Armstrong began, "When I was assigned to the Lynwood Station as a trainee, I met a group of officers who had been frustrated for years with how hard it was to put away drug dealers. One time they all went out and got drunk and got identical tattoos on the right calf of their leg."

"It wouldn't be my choice of how to spend my time-off, but there's nothing against the law about getting a tattoo."

"It wasn't the tattoo," Armstrong said. "It was what it stood for."

"What did it stand for?"

"The tattoo was of a Viking warrior. Vikings are known for taking matters into their own hands. That's what these guys did."

"How?" Dutton asked.

"They made an agreement to plant evidence, and to lie whenever necessary on their reports, if it meant being able to put away some known, sleazeball drug dealer.

"Sometimes they'd grab someone they thought was a drug dealer and just beat him up."

"Somebody must have found out they were doing that."

"Nobody did."

"Why didn't you report them?" Dutton asked.

"I was new. I thought that was the way we were supposed to do things. So I joined their group and began to do whatever they said."

Now Dutton was the one who was depressed. He reached for a piece of chocolate and put it in his mouth.

Armstrong continued. "I might have gone on that way for the rest of my career, but then I was transferred to the San Dimas Station. I wanted to fit in and be thought of as a good officer. One night a group of us stopped for coffee. They started talking about a crack house. They'd reported it to narcotics weeks before, but nothing had happened. I told 'em, 'Well, in the Lynwood Station, we'd have taken care of it in one night.' They asked me how and I said, 'Watch this.'"

Armstrong closed his eyes and shook his head. "I should've kept my mouth shut. But I didn't. I called the station and gave an address just across the street from the crack house. I said I could hear gun shots coming from the house. Right away that created an exception to a search warrant. A minute later we got a call to go to the crack house. When we pulled up, I went to the door and started banging on it, yelling for them to open up.

"I figured they'd run out the back door, leaving the drugs and the money. We'd gather 'em up, take 'em back to the station, and become instant heroes. But it didn't work that way. The drug dealer didn't stay there at night. He took the money and the drugs and left his woman there. When she heard me banging on the door, she thought it was an unsatisfied customer, so she grabbed a rifle that didn't even work. She thought if she opened the door and pointed the gun, whoever it was would get the hint and come back in the morning. So when she opened the door, and I saw the weapon, I fired in self-defense. I shot the woman, terminating the fetus, and ended up getting second-degree jail time for it."

"It's a bad deal. I'm really sorry."

"Not as sorry as I am."

"Please tell me it isn't true what you said about the Vikings though."

Armstrong reached down and pulled up his right pant leg, showing Dutton a tattoo of a Viking.

"Would you be willing to tell this to the sheriff or someone who works in his office?" Dutton asked.

He shrugged his shoulders. "What have I got to lose now?"

Dutton got on the phone and called John Buehler. "I've been talking to Armstrong. You've got to come out and listen to his story."

It took two hours but finally Buehler showed up.

At two-thirty that afternoon, as Dutton and Buehler talked in the parking lot, Dutton asked, "What do we do now?"

"I'm not sure. What do you suggest?"

"I think we need to go through the Lynwood Station and fire anyone with a Viking tattoo on their right leg."

Buehler smiled. "On what grounds?"

"We can build a case."

"I wish life were that simple, Dutton, but I'll tell you what I'll do. I'll pass this on up the line, and see what they want to do with it."

On the way back to his office, Henderson called him on his cell phone.

"What's up?" Dutton asked.

"I got a phone call Sunday from Billingsley from L.A. Narcotics. They were set up to do a raid on a money house. But when they showed up, they found a man dead from a gunshot wound. The neighbors said some cops had already beaten them to it. So they're trying to find out who did the first raid. Do your people know anything about this?"

"We don't do drug raids. You know that. Probably federal. They never talk to us mere earthlings."

"Billingsley said he checked. It wasn't them."

"Not us either."

"Then who was it?"

"Maybe some cops from another town. When they make a report, we'll know who it was."

"I've called around. Nobody seems to know anything about it."

"It'll sort itself out," Dutton said.

Wednesday, February 26

Dutton phoned Buehler. "What have you guys decided to do about the Vikings?"

"It's still under review."

"We need to move on this right away. A group like this can poison the whole force. What's taking so long?"

"It hasn't been that long."

"It shouldn't have taken even a day. Don't you people understand that we've got a very serious problem here? Right now it's localized, and we can deal with it. But if it gets into other stations, it could bring down the entire sheriff's department."

"I'll get back to you as soon as a decision is made. That's all I can say."

As soon as he hung up, Dutton wrote a report summarizing everything Armstrong had told him, and about his dealings with Buehler. He sent it to headquarters and kept two copies for himself. One he filed at the station and the other he would take home for safekeeping. He wanted a permanent record that he could use in case Buehler later said he couldn't remember any discussion he'd had with Dutton about the Vikings.

Whatever happened, Dutton was not willing to be held responsible for sitting on information that should have been reported to his superiors.

*   *   *

Not all drug dealers go to jail. Sometimes a small dealer can be persuaded to become an informant instead of serving jail time.

Early in March, NORSAT developed an informant who told them about the Monkey Boys and their activities, even identifying the four gang members by name. NORSAT immediately began a round-the-clock surveillance of Chad Nieteri and his three friends.

A week later, Dutton reviewed the surveillance report and learned that Chad Nieteri's girlfriend was from Ashton, Idaho. *Idaho? I wonder if she's LDS,* he thought. *If she is, how did she ever get involved in this?*

Friday, March 21

"Come on in," Chad said. "I'll put in the pizza, and you start the movie."

It was past midnight. Earlier Kristen had been with Chad and his friends at a bar. They had all agreed to meet after to watch a movie at Chad's apartment.

Kristen hesitated at the doorway. She felt a strong impression she shouldn't be there.

"Anything wrong?" Chad asked.

"When are the others coming?"

"Any minute."

As she stepped inside and Chad closed the door, she felt what could only be described as an evil influence. She felt as though she could hardly breathe.

At the same time, in the parking lot, Officer Beckman, sitting in what appeared to be a plumbing contractor's van, jotted on a notepad. "12:10 A.M. Nieteri and Boone enter Nieteri's apartment." He yawned and sat back.

In the kitchen, Chad slid a frozen pizza into the oven. "So much for my clean oven, right?"

He joined her in the living room. "You want to start the movie?" he asked.

"I guess."

"I'll do it." He started the movie then sat next to her on the couch.

While they watched the movie, Kristen kept looking at the clock. "When are they coming?"

"They probably stopped off to get something. Mike doesn't like pizza."

A short time later he leaned over and kissed her.

"No," she said softly.

"Why not? We're friends aren't we?" he asked.

"I shouldn't be here alone with you."

"The others will be here any minute," he said.

"I don't feel good about this."

"Don't you like me?"

"I do. I like you very much. But . . ."

"What?"

She couldn't tell him that she didn't trust him because that seemed like such a cruel thing to say. After all he'd done for her, she didn't want to hurt his feelings. "I don't know. It's probably nothing."

They watched the movie until the timer for the pizza dinged.

"I'll take care of it," Chad said softly. "You just relax."

He removed the pizza from the oven and set it on the coffee table in front of them. Then he opened a couple of beers and set them next to the pizza.

She wasn't hungry, but she had one slice of pizza.

"You're not drinking?" Chad asked.

She didn't trust herself alone with Chad. "No, I'm okay."

"Suit yourself. I'll drink yours as soon as I finish mine."

They settled back on the couch to watch the movie when Chad leaned over and kissed her again. From then on it seemed to be just one very long sustained kiss. After a while, she couldn't think clearly.

"Let's go into my room where we'll be more comfortable," he whispered in her ear.

The suggestion jolted her back to reality. She stood up. "Where are Mike and Summer? Where is everybody? You said they were all coming, so where are they?"

"Forget them, okay? C'mon, I'm crazy about you. You know this is what we both want."

She hurried to the front door. "I can't stay here."

He caught up with her and grabbed her arm. "What is wrong with you?"

"Let me go."

"Do you have any idea how much money I've spent on you? And have I ever asked for anything in return? No, I have not. But let me tell you something, I'm only human. I have certain needs. It's as simple as that."

"What are you talking about?" she asked.

"You know what I'm talking about."

"I can't do . . . that," she said.

"Why not?" he asked.

"I just can't."

"Hey, you owe me! No one crosses Chad Nieteri!" A darkness came over his face that made Kristen shiver.

"Please let me go, Chad," she begged.

In a rage, he turned away from her and flung the pizza off the coffee table. "Fine then! Who needs you? Get out of here and quit wasting my time!" He called her a vulgar name and glared at her.

She bolted through the door and ran down the stairs. Tears stung her eyes, and she was trembling.

Beckman saw her leave. He wrote on his pad. "Boone leaves in a hurry at 1:32 A.M." He couldn't help but worry about the girl, so he had her shadowed until she caught a cab back to her apartment.

Wednesday, March 26

A few days later, Jonathan caught up to Kristen on her way to class. "You okay? You weren't at institute last night."

"I know. Sorry. I'll be there next week for sure."

"Everything okay?" he asked.

"I'll tell you about it on Sunday. Will you pick me up for church?"

"Yeah, sure."

As they approached her classroom building, she noticed Chad standing by some trees watching her. She gasped involuntarily.

"What's wrong?" Jonathan asked.

"There's a guy on my right by those trees. Don't make it obvious you're looking at him."

Jonathan dropped his book. As he bent over to pick it up, he spotted Chad.

They continued on their way. "What about him?"

"His name is Chad Nieteri. I have been seeing him off and on, but not anymore. I found out I couldn't trust him."

"Anything I can do for you?"

"No, it's all taken care of. It's just that I can hardly wait to get back to my boring life."

After class, Chad caught up with her. He tried to hand her a cup of hot chocolate but she wouldn't take it.

"I have to go." She turned and walked away.

He moved past her and stopped, facing her. He held his free hand up, his palm facing her. "Look, I came to apologize for the way I acted. I was totally off base, and I've resolved to do better. I've quit drinking for good."

"I can't talk to you."

"I know, but, look, I've met with the missionaries a couple times since that night. And I'm even thinking about getting baptized."

She hesitated. "Really?"

"I am. You've been such a good example for me. So if I could just spend a little more time with you, that's all it would take."

She wondered if he was lying. "It's too late for that." Once again, she started to walk away.

He kept in front of her, backpedaling. "Please, Kristen, give me one more chance. Let me prove to you how much I've changed."

What if he really has changed? she asked herself.

She looked into his face, trying to gauge his sincerity.

"At least talk with me long enough to finish your hot chocolate," he said with a smile, holding out the cup again.

She reached for the cup.

"That's my girl!"

In the student cafeteria, as they sat and talked, he was his most charming self. He made her laugh. He asked about her classes. He invited her to go with him and his friends on Saturday to Marina Del Ray where they'd go sailing.

"I like it when you're like this," she said.

"You're right. I don't know what happened the other night. I must have had too much to drink, but that will never happen again."

She wanted to believe him.

"Oh, I almost forgot. Mike's uncle will be in town in the next week or two. He's looking forward to meeting you and doing the screen test."

"Really? That is good news."

They fell into the same pattern of lighthearted talk they'd enjoyed before. Even though she was taking part in it just as usual, a thought kept

/

nagging at her—*What if the temper and the demands are the real Chad? What if the things Chad said to me Friday night about his physical needs reflect who he really is? What if this whole thing has been one big, elaborate setup?*

"Can I ask you a question?" she said.

"Of course."

"Do you always blow up when you don't get your way?"

He gave her a sheepish look. "Like I said, I must have had too much to drink."

"Does that mean you take no responsibility for your actions when you drink? That must be convenient for you."

"I don't normally have a temper. I don't know what happened. Ask my friends. They'll all tell you how hard it is to get me mad."

"How do I know I can trust your friends?"

"You can trust Summer, can't you?"

She thought about it. "Yes, I think so."

"Then ask her about me the next time you see her."

"All right, I just might do that."

I don't know any more than I did before, she thought. Suddenly she thought of a way to find out what Chad was really like. "What's the most impressive thing you've learned from the missionaries?"

He turned his head away and stared outside for a minute, and then relaxed and with a smile said, "Well, there's so many things one could talk about, isn't there?"

"Yes, of course. Give me one."

"Well, there's the Book of Mormon . . . and . . . uh . . . Joseph Smith," he said.

"What has impressed you the most from your reading of the Book of Mormon?"

"Why are you asking me these questions? Don't you trust me?"

"I'm just curious, that's all."

"It doesn't feel like curiosity."

"How many pages have you read?"

"I can't say for sure."

"What are the names of the missionaries you're meeting with?"

He began tapping his fingers on the table. "I really don't appreciate you grilling me like this."

It was then she saw in his eyes the same anger she'd seen the night she'd walked out of his apartment. *That's who he really is,* she thought.

Now that she knew what he was really like, she didn't want to make him mad. She just wanted to get away from him and never see him again. She broke into a smile. "You're right, Chad. Sorry. What were we talking about before I became the grand inquisitor?"

He smiled. "For a moment there, I was afraid I was going to need a lawyer."

The next few minutes should have been fun. Kristen played the part but could hardly wait to leave. "I need to go study," she said finally.

"What about us going sailing Saturday?"

"You know that sounds like so much fun, but I need to work on a term paper."

"For what class?" he asked.

"Now who's being the grand inquisitor?"

"You're right. Well, okay, I'll miss you. I'll take pictures and tell you all about it on Monday."

"I'll look forward to it."

*　　*　　*

On Saturday afternoon, she called Jonathan's apartment to remind him to pick her up for church. His roommate told her that the night before Jonathan had been attacked in the parking lot of his apartment, and that he was in the hospital.

She hurried to the hospital to see him.

As she entered his hospital room, she could see that his face was bruised and puffy, and there was an ugly, stitched-up gash above his right eyebrow, and that he had a cast on his left arm.

"Jonathan, I came as soon as I heard. What happened?"

"These two guys jumped me from behind. I didn't even have a chance." His lips were swollen, and he had a hard time speaking.

"Oh, Jonathan, I'm so sorry."

He dropped his gaze for a minute without speaking. Then he lifted his eyes. "He was there. I saw him, sitting in a car."

"Who?" Kristen asked.

"That Chad guy," Jonathan answered. "What are you doing, Kristen, getting mixed up with someone like him?"

She talked with Jonathan for a few more minutes, then drove slowly back to her apartment. At first she thought about leaving L.A. and going home to Idaho. She was afraid. Afraid of what Chad was capable of doing. But after thinking about it for a while, she began to wonder if she might not be judging Chad unfairly. *So what if he lost his temper? Everyone gets mad occasionally. And it's horrible what happened to Jonathan, but maybe he was mistaken about seeing Chad watching him get beat up. Jonathan only saw him that once on campus. How could he be so sure it was Chad in the car? Besides, Chad really can be fun. Like he was that first day when we all went swimming. And like he was again yesterday in the cafeteria.*

She was about to put leaving for home out of her mind, when she thought about Mike's girlfriend, Summer. Chad had suggested she call Summer, and suddenly that felt like a good idea. Summer was a drop-dead gorgeous girl, but Kristen remembered Mike not wanting her to know about Kristen's screen test. He'd made some excuse about her not understanding why Kristen would be getting favored treatment. She wondered just how loyal Summer might be to Mike and the others.

Kristen dug around in her backpack and found the notebook where she had written down the other girls' phone numbers. There were two for Summer—one at her apartment and the other a cellphone. She tried the cellphone number first.

"Hello?"

"Summer? Hey, this is Kristen. How's it going?"

"Great! I just got off work and I'm on my way to the gym. What's up?"

"Well, this is kind of awkward, but I need to ask you something. Are you someplace you can talk?"

"Sure. Is something wrong?"

"This is going to sound really stupid . . . but . . . how well do you really know Chad Nieteri?"

"I don't know. Pretty well. Why do you ask?"

"It's just that I feel like our relationship is moving along pretty fast, and I . . . I need to know if I can trust him, like I want to."

"Hang on a second, I'm just pulling into the parking lot at my gym."

The phone went dead for a minute, and it occurred to Kristen how silly she must be sounding.

Summer came back on the line. "Okay. What is it you want to know?"

"Nothing. You know, this was a bad idea. Just forget I called."

"No, hang on."

Kristen heard Summer take a deep breath before she said, "I probably shouldn't say this, because if Chad ever found out, he'd . . . "

"He'd what?" Kristen asked.

"Well, let's just say that would be the end of the free ride for me." She paused, then said, "Look, you seem like a really nice kid, and from the beginning I wondered what you were doing going out with Chad."

"Why? Is there something wrong with him?" Kristen had a feeling she was going to hear something she didn't want to know.

"Let me put it this way, and I'll deny it if you ever tell anyone what I'm going to say. The truth is, Chad is not what he pretends to be. He plays rough, and Mike has told me some things Chad has done to the girls he breaks up with. It's something a girl like you shouldn't have to go through."

"What do you mean?" Kristen asked.

"I've probably said too much," Summer said. "But if I were you, I'd watch my back." With that she hung up, leaving Kristen feeling numb.

But it was suddenly clear what she needed to do. The things she had suspected about him were true, and she needed to get away from Chad and out of L.A. Without giving any thought to school or the lease on her apartment or anything else, she quickly packed up her things, shoved them in her car, and drove away.

There was only one place of safety for her now, and that was back home in Idaho.

CHAPTER SIX

Dutton looked around the room at the men who were coordinating the Monkey Boy investigation. Archibald, with his wrinkled shirt and loosened tie, looked like he hadn't slept for a week. With his rumpled gray sport coat slung over the back of his chair, his shoulder holster was clearly in view. He was responsible for the surveillance component of the investigation.

They'd been meeting all morning but were taking time out for a break—coffee and donuts for all the others, and milk and donuts for Dutton. Dutton's secretary, Delilah, had once sheepishly confessed that behind his back some of Dutton's men called him Moo-Cow.

"We can confirm that the Boone girl is now at her folks' home in Idaho," Archibald said.

"Why did she go home?" Dutton asked.

"Can't say yet. We do know she packed up and left in an awful hurry after visiting a friend in the hospital." He looked at some papers on his clipboard. "Jonathan Yearsley."

"Why was he in the hospital?" Dutton asked.

"He got beat up."

"Who did it?"

"We're working on that. But we do know that Nieteri drove up, parked, stayed in his car, watched a little of it, and then drove off."

"Did he communicate with any of the thugs?" Dutton asked.

"No, he just drove up, stopped, watched, and drove away. You want us to bring in the goons who did it?"

Dutton shook his head. "Not yet. We don't want Nieteri to know we're tailing him." His gaze fixed on one of the donuts still on the tray. He wanted it badly, but Laura had talked him into going on a diet with her. She'd lost five pounds but, so far, he hadn't lost anything.

"So Kristen Boone leaves after visiting Jonathan Yearsley in the hospital. Did she drop her classes?"

"No, she just packed up and left."

Dutton slid the donut box away from him. "I think I'll go talk to her."

*   *   *

That afternoon Dutton took a flight to Salt Lake City, then caught another flight to Idaho Falls, where he rented a car. He stayed the night in a hotel in Idaho Falls.

The next morning he drove to Ashton, about an hour away. The Boone family lived five miles west of town on a small farm.

Dutton knocked on the door a little after eight in the morning. A big-boned man with large, work-hardened hands opened the door. "What can I do for you?" he asked.

"Mr. Boone?"

"That's right."

Dutton showed him his badge. "Sir, I'm Kendall Dutton. I'm with a special investigative unit of the Los Angeles County Sheriff's Department. I would like to have a few words with your daughter Kristen."

"Is she in trouble?"

"No, sir, not at all. I just need to ask her a few questions."

"Come in."

Dutton stepped inside. It was an older house. The furniture was out-of-date but not enough to be considered antique.

"She's probably still asleep," Mr. Boone said.

"Would you mind waking her up?"

"I'll go get her."

"Thank you."

Five minutes later Kristen came into the room, barefoot, wearing faded blue jeans and an oversized T-shirt. Her hair had been tied back in a thick ponytail, and she had a confused look on her face. "My dad said you wanted to talk to me."

"Yes. Sorry to get you out of bed."

"That's okay. I needed to get up anyway."

"My name is Officer Dutton. I'm with the Los Angeles County Sheriff's Department. I'd like to ask you a few questions."

They were still standing facing each other in the living room. "What about?"

"Could we sit down?" Dutton asked.

"Oh, yes, of course. I'm sorry."

She sat as far away as she could and still be in the same room.

I need to win her trust, Dutton thought. He spotted an *Ensign* magazine on their coffee table.

"I was reading the *Ensign* on the plane. There's a great article about the Book of Mormon."

Dutton experienced a twinge of guilt. The truth was he hadn't brought his *Ensign* on the plane, but he had read the issue a few days earlier.

"Are you LDS?" she asked.

"I am. In my ward I work with the priests quorum. My wife is the Laurel adviser. We have three kids. I have their pictures here if you'd like to see what they look like."

She came over and sat down on the far end of the couch where he was seated. He showed her a picture of his family and told her a little about each one.

"They're good kids," he said. "I'll be glad to get back home again. Which brings me back to why I'm here." He slipped his wallet back into his pocket. "I've been told you know Chad Nieteri. I need some information about him."

Kristen cringed at hearing Chad's name, but she said nothing, waiting for Dutton to go on.

Kristen's dad entered the room and sat down.

"Dad, you don't have to be here," she said. "I'm okay, really."

"You sure?"

"Positive. I just found out that Mr. Dutton is a member of the Church."

Her dad smiled. "Is that right? Small world, isn't it? Of course up here, it isn't that unusual to bump into someone who's a member, but I'd guess that's not true in Los Angeles."

"That's right," Dutton said.

"Well, okay, I've got a few projects around the house that I need to work on. If you need me, Kristen, I'll be in the kitchen." With that, he left.

"You want to take a walk?" Kristen said. "It's a nice day . . . and I won't have to worry if my folks are listening in."

"I'm all for a walk."

Kristen excused herself long enough to put on a pair of shoes, then they left the house and started walking along the gravel drive that led to the highway.

"Officer Dutton, what has Chad done that brings you all the way up here to talk to me?" she asked.

"I'm not sure he's done anything. I'm just following up on some leads, that's all."

"In other words, you're not going to tell me, right?"

Dutton ignored the question. "How long have you known Chad?"

"Only a couple of months. He was in one of my classes, or at least I thought he was. After a while though, he quit coming to class. So I'm not really sure if he was in the class or not."

"Did you ever see him after class?"

"Yes, I did. At first just to talk, and then we started hanging out together as friends. That's all, just friends."

"What's he like?" Dutton asked.

"He's smart and very sure of himself. Fun to be with sometimes. But he has a bad temper too."

"Did you ever meet any of his friends?"

"Oh, sure," Kristen said. "We hung out with them."

"What were they like?"

"They were a lot of fun."

"Did Chad ever mention his dad?" Dutton asked.

"His dad is a policeman, isn't he?"

"Yes, that's right."

"Other than that, he didn't talk about his dad much."

"Why did you quit school and come up here?" he asked.

"Well, to tell you the truth, I was scared."

"Of Chad?"

"Yes. At first he was fun to be with. And very generous."

"In what way?"

"Well, just a day or two after I met him, he tried to give me a new laptop. I didn't take it because I didn't feel right about it, but then later he gave me his old laptop. He told me he was going to throw it out if I didn't want it, so I took it."

Dutton stopped walking. "You have his old laptop?"

"Yes."

"Here?"

"Yes."

"I'd very much like to have our computer experts see what he's got on it."

"Well, I doubt if it would do you any good. He told me he erased all his files."

"We have some very clever people who can retrieve whatever was saved on a computer. I have no idea how they do it. Would it be all right with you if I take the laptop with me when I go?"

"Yeah, I guess so. I've never used it."

"In what other ways was Chad generous?"

"He and his three friends would take four of us girls to expensive places to eat. They always seemed to have lots of money to throw around."

"When did you first begin to be suspicious of Chad?" Dutton asked.

She began to blush. "This is hard to talk about. But, anyway, one night after we'd been to a bar, we all agreed to go to Chad's place to watch a movie, but the others never showed up, and . . . well, nothing happened. I mean, not really. Or at least not what you think."

"Something must have happened."

"This is really embarrassing to talk about to a stranger."

"I understand."

"The minute I stepped inside his place, I had the feeling that I shouldn't be there. I know that sounds crazy, but it's the way I felt."

"So you left?"

"I wish I had. No, I told myself I was imagining it. We started . . . kissing, but that's all. And a few minutes later Chad asked me to go into the bedroom with him. I wouldn't do it, and we got in this big argument."

"What did he say?"

"He told me I owed him because of all the money he'd spent on me. He starts yelling at me. He says nobody crosses Chad Nieteri. Until then I didn't know what a bad temper he has. He swore at me and knocked a pizza on the floor. It was scary. I'm so glad I got out of there." She brushed away some tears rolling down her cheek.

"You okay?" he asked.

"Sorry."

"Is that why you left town—because of the way he reacted when you wouldn't stay the night with him?"

"No. Chad saw me with a friend from institute. Chad must have been jealous because I think he had some of his friends beat Jonathan up."

"What's Jonathan's last name?"

"Yearsley."

Even though he knew about Jonathan, he wrote it down for her benefit.

"Why do you think Chad had anything to do with Jonathan getting beat up?" Dutton asked.

"Jonathan saw Chad in a car watching it happen."

"Did Jonathan tell you that?" Dutton asked.

"Yes, in the hospital, but for a little while, I didn't want to believe it. That's when I decided to call Summer."

"Summer?"

"Yeah, she's the girlfriend of Mike Collins, one of Chad's buddies."

"What did she tell you?"

"She said that Chad isn't what he pretends to be and hinted that some of his girlfriends had ended up hurt."

"Physically?"

"That's what it sounded like. Anyway, after she told me that, I freaked out and packed up and left."

"Has Chad tried to contact you since you've been here?" Dutton asked.

"He's sent me some e-mails, but I haven't answered any of them."

"What did he say in his e-mails?" Dutton asked.

"That he misses me and wishes that I had talked to him before I left. What do you think I should do?"

Dutton took a deep breath. "Look, I've got reason to believe Chad is a dangerous person. I'd suggest you answer his e-mails. Let him know you're just up here for a while and then you're going back. Like maybe someone in your family got sick."

"What good will that do?" she asked.

"Buy you some time," Dutton said.

Her dad came out of the house. "Mr. Dutton, have you had breakfast yet? We'd like you to stay and eat with us."

"Well, thanks for the offer but I probably should be going. I have to get to Idaho Falls and catch my flight."

"What time is your flight?"

"Three o'clock."

"You've got plenty of time," he said. "We'll be eating in about fifteen minutes."

Dutton hesitated. "Well, that's very kind of you, but . . . where I come from, folks don't usually extend breakfast invitations to cops who drop by their house."

"People are friendlier here. Besides, you've got to eat, right? You might as well do it here."

"All right. Thank you very much."

While they were eating, there was an uncomfortable silence. Dutton looked at Kristen, thinking she might say something to her parents about why he had come all the way from California, but she didn't.

After he cleaned off his plate, Kristen's mother asked, "Won't you have some more bacon or fried potatoes, Mr. Dutton?"

"Oh, no thanks. I'm full as a toad. It was wonderful."

They all fell silent again. After a moment, Dutton said, "Look, I don't know what you know about why Kristen dropped out of school. I take it she hasn't said much. She's not in trouble with the police, but she has some information about someone the police have an interest in. I came here to find out what she knows."

Kristen's mom covered her mouth with her hand and looked concerned. Rulon Boone looked at his daughter and said, "Kristen, is there something you need to tell us?"

Kristen shook her head and for a moment didn't respond, then, looking at Dutton she said, "I met this guy at school. His name is Chad. I don't need to give you all the details, but he wasn't what he pretended to be, and I . . . I was afraid he might hurt me."

"Oh, honey," her mom said, "why didn't you tell us?"

Kristen sighed. "I just didn't want to talk about it."

Dutton cleared his throat, "Well, that was a mighty fine meal. Beats the donuts and milk I usually have for breakfast. Cop food, you know." He put his napkin on the table and stood. "But now, I really do need to get going."

Just then the phone rang. Kristen's mom answered it. Dutton could tell right away it wasn't good.

"No, she's not here right now. Who is this?"

Mrs. Boone motioned for Dutton to come to her. She wrote on a pad of paper near the phone. "It's Chad. He wants to talk to Kristen."

Dutton grabbed the pad and wrote: "She went to the store. She'll be back in about twenty minutes."

"She's out now," Mrs. Boone said. "She went to the store. I expect she'll be back in about twenty minutes . . . All right . . . Thank you. Good-bye." She hung up the phone.

By then Kristen was pacing the floor. "Why did you have my mom say I'd be back in twenty minutes?" she asked Dutton.

"We need time to work out what you're going to tell Chad."

"What am I going to tell him?"

"What would bring you up here without giving him notice?" Dutton asked.

"Well, my sister Amber just had a baby. I could have come up here to help her out. She has two other kids that are a handful."

"That will work. Tell him that. And tell him as soon as she's back on her feet, you'll be returning to California. Also, I want you to tell him you've really been missing him, and that you were going to call but you've just been so busy with Amber's kids, you haven't had a chance."

"Why would I tell him that?"

"So he won't get worried and come up here looking for you."

"Do you think he would do that? I'm not going back to him."

"No, you're not. At the end of the week, you'll tell him Amber is still having a rough time, and her husband is working out-of-state and isn't able to help around the house, so you're going to stay a little longer."

"And then what?"

"Keep him thinking you're about to go back. That will keep him from coming up here."

"I'm not in the habit of lying."

"Sometimes it's necessary, if it saves lives."

"You have a very warped outlook on life," Kristen said.

"It comes from working with the worst layers of society."

Her dad spoke up. "Kristen, I don't know everything that's been going on, but he's the expert. I think you should do what he says."

Kristen thought about it. "All right, but I'm going to need some help."

Over the next few minutes, they laid out any details she might need in talking to Chad.

Chad called exactly twenty minutes later. Kristen answered it.

"Oh, Chad, my mom told me you called! How's it going?"

As Kristen listened to Chad, she put her hand over the mouthpiece and shook her head. "I can't do this," she whispered to Dutton.

"You have to do it to keep him from coming up here," he said softly.

Kristen spent the first few minutes explaining to Chad that Amber needed her, and that she hadn't had time to talk to him before she left. The one thing that set alarm bells going off in Dutton's mind was that Chad got Amber's last name from Kristen.

"I didn't want to bother you at work," she said.

Pause.

"No, I wasn't running away from you. Why would I do that? Look, Amber is getting stronger every day. I really think I'll be leaving here in maybe a week."

She stole a sideways glance at her mom. "I miss you too, Chad. Very much . . . Yes, I still have your old laptop. I brought it up here to learn how to use it. So far all I've done is play solitaire on it every night. . . . Okay, I'll bring it with me when I come back."

Kristen grabbed a tissue and wiped her forehead.

"You want to call Amber? Why? To check up on me? Now who's

playing grand inquisitor? Look, if you don't believe me, come up here and stay a few days. I'd love to show you around."

Dutton winced.

She continued. "In fact, actually, that might be good. It will give you a chance to meet my family. They're very anxious to meet you. You know, just in case we get serious. I know we haven't talked about it, but, gosh, the way things are going with you taking the missionary lessons, and how much fun we have together, I really think that's a possibility, don't you?"

She paused while he replied and then said, "I miss you too, Chad . . . Yes, you too. Bye."

After hanging up, she sank down on the couch and put her hands to her face. Dutton sat down next to her.

She stood up. "Can we take another walk?"

Once they got outside, she said, "I messed up, didn't I?"

"No, you did well."

"I shouldn't have invited him up here."

"I think it will work to our advantage. Now he'll think you want to marry him. My guess is he's not the marrying kind."

"He's not."

"So what you said will probably keep him away. It may have been the best thing you could have said."

She looked at Dutton gratefully. "Thanks for helping me."

"I hope I helped."

"You did."

"I need to go now," he said.

"Can't you take a later flight, in case he calls again?"

"I really need to get back."

"Please. The thing is, I can't talk to my folks about what to say. Their advice has always been to tell the truth. They're not as good at lying as you are."

Dutton smiled. "Thanks, I guess."

"Oh, you know what I mean. It's because of your job, not some character defect. Can't you take a later flight? That way we can go talk to Amber in case Chad calls her."

He thought about it. "All right. It will probably be helpful to talk to her."

"Thank you. I'll go tell my folks."

Kristen and Dutton drove to Amber's place to work out a story in case Chad called her. They returned around noon.

Kristen's folks insisted that Dutton eat lunch with them. He asked questions about their life. They were only too eager to tell him about their friends, neighbors, ward members, and local events. None of it was very exciting but somehow it appealed to Dutton because it was a small town with small problems.

At twelve-thirty, just as Dutton was getting into his car to leave, Amber drove into the driveway, blocking Dutton's car.

"Chad called!" Amber said. "He started asking questions. I didn't know what to say. I'm not very good at this sort of thing."

"What did you say?"

"Let's go inside. We need to let Kristen in on this."

Dutton looked at his watch, sighed, and then helped Amber get her kids out of the car and followed her into the house.

"Chad called," Amber told Kristen and their folks. "He asked me a bunch of questions."

"Tell us what he asked and what you said," Dutton urged.

"He asked if I was Kristen's sister. I told him yes and then he told me his name and that he and Kristen were seeing each other. He asked me if I'd just had a baby. I told him yes. He asked me how old the baby was, and I panicked."

"You don't know how old your baby is?" Dutton asked.

"No, that's not it. I didn't know what Kristen told him."

"Kristen, did you tell Chad how old the baby is?" Dutton asked.

"I did. I said Amber had her baby a couple of weeks ago."

"Amber, when did you have your baby?" Dutton asked.

"It's over three weeks ago. In three more days it will be a month."

"I think that's close enough," Dutton said.

"But don't you see?" Amber said. "We should have agreed on everything. It isn't fair to ask me to make things up that aren't true."

"What else did he ask?" Kristen wondered.

"He asked where you were. I said you'd gone to the store and that you'd be back in a few minutes. He said he'd call back. Kristen, you've got to be there when he calls or he'll start thinking we're lying."

"Anything else?" Dutton asked.

"No."

"I don't think you said anything that would make him doubt our story," Dutton said.

"But what if he calls again? What if he starts demanding a bunch of answers that I don't know? Who is this guy, and what has he done that would bring a policeman all the way from Los Angeles? Has he killed someone? If he's done something wrong why don't you just arrest him, instead of putting my family in danger?"

"He's just someone we're interested in, that's all."

"Don't do that to us," Kristen complained. "I know that police are always talking about someone being a person of interest, but our lives may be in danger. You can at least tell us what you think he may have done."

Dutton sighed. "All right. If we press charges, it will be for racketeering, impersonating a police officer, assaulting drug dealers, arranging to have Jonathan beaten up, and murder."

"Kristen, what have you gotten us into?" Amber gasped. She turned to Dutton. "If he comes up here to kill Kristen, there wouldn't be a thing any of us could do to stop him!" Her voice was rising, and she was very nearly hysterical.

"It's true that Kristen might be in danger if Chad suspects something, but you can protect her if you'll just calm down," Dutton said.

"Calm down?" Amber shouted. "How can I calm down? It's not just me. I have my kids to think about. And what if I don't want to do this? Why can't Kristen just go away so we're not in danger?" She was in tears.

"Then Chad will be suspicious, and if he's the one we're looking for, he might try to find her and hurt her. Our best bet is to keep him assured that Kristen is up here to help you."

Amber went outside to complain to her dad, who was playing with her kids. A few minutes later she came back. "I guess I'll do it."

"You can do it, Amber. I'm sure of it. And I'll leave you my cell phone number in case you have any questions."

Dutton said his good-byes. Kristen went with him out to his car. "Kristen, I'm not sure how this is going to turn out, but it's possible that if this goes to trial, you might be asked to testify."

"Testify? About what?"

"The things you've told me."

"What would the media say about me? That I was his girlfriend?"

"I don't know," Dutton said. "I have no control over what the media does."

"Please leave me out of this."

"Look, I'm just a cop. I don't make decisions like that. But the truth is, if the laptop has any evidence stored on it, you may have to testify. I'm sorry."

She started sobbing. Her mom came out of the house and hurried to her side and put her arms around her. "What did you say to her?"

"I told her she may have to testify if this goes to trial." He looked at his watch. "Sorry, but I really need to go if I'm going to catch my plane."

Her mother glared at him. "Go then. You've done enough damage here for one day."

Dutton got in his car and drove away. As he left, he could see Kristen being led back to the house by her mom.

His flight landed in L.A. at 8:30 P.M., and an hour later he pulled into his driveway and went inside the house.

"I'm home!"

Gabe, his four-year-old, came running out of his bedroom and into his dad's arms. He picked him up and hugged him.

"Hey, big guy, I missed you! What's happening?"

"We went to McDonald's, and I had a Happy Meal!"

"What a day for you! Did you go down the slide?"

"Uh-huh! And I didn't even get hurt."

"Good for you."

He carried Gabe into the kitchen.

"Daddy's home!" Gabe proudly announced.

"I can see that!" Laura said, giving Dutton a kiss. "How was your trip?"

"It was okay. Where's Abigail and Adam?"

"In their rooms."

He went to say hello to his kids. A few minutes later Dutton returned to the kitchen, where Laura was paying some bills.

"Oh, we got you a Happy Meal," Laura said. "Gabe insisted we get you one. That's why he's still up. He wanted to make sure you got it."

"A Happy Meal for me? Thanks, Gabe!"

Gabe led him to the refrigerator and gave him a sack. "I got it just for you, Daddy!"

"Thank you! How did you know I was in the mood for a Happy Meal?"

Gabe smiled. "I just did, that's all."

"Well, come and help me eat it, okay?" He heated the hamburger and fries in the microwave, poured a glass of milk, and they sat down together.

"Why did you have to go away?" Gabe asked.

"Police business."

"Were you trying to catch some bad guys?"

"Yes, that's my job."

From his single days, Dutton had had about as many McDonald's fries as anyone should ever have to eat, but with Gabe watching, he had to eat some. He cut the hamburger into halves, hoping he could talk Gabe into sharing it. But Gabe really did want Dutton to have it all. And so he did.

Gabe did help him with the fries though.

They had a good time talking with each other, and then about twenty minutes later Laura came in from the laundry room. "We need to get you guys to bed. It's way past your bedtime. Go tell Abigail and Adam it's time for family prayer."

They had family prayer, and then Laura and Dutton each hugged their kids and told them they loved them and sent them off to bed—a process that generally took about twenty minutes, what with Gabe's insistance on drinks, snacks, delays, and diversions.

And then they were alone and could talk.

"How was your flight?" she asked.

"It was okay."

"I still don't understand why you had to go to Idaho."

"I needed to talk to someone."

"Do you still feel like if you catch this one crook, then that will be the end of all crime?"

"I don't believe that," he said.

"I think you do. That's why you're such a good cop. But sometimes . . . when you're not around, it's hard for your kids."

"I can usually choose my hours. This may never happen again."

She reached for his hand. "I complain too much, don't I?"

"No, not at all. There's nobody who's as understanding about what it means to have a cop for a husband as you."

"I love you. That's why. A part of me wishes you had a boring eight-to-five job, and another part of me is proud of the way you've dedicated your life to making us all safer."

She got up, put the milk back in the refrigerator, looked around for anything else that needed to be done, and then said, "I'm done complaining." She kissed him on the cheek. "Welcome home, Idaho cowboy."

CHAPTER SEVEN

Wednesday, April 9, 12:30 A.M.; Ashton, Idaho

Kristen couldn't sleep.

She sat in the darkness on a lawn chair near some trees at the edge of their property, wishing she had brought a blanket out with her and watching for cars on the highway. There was little traffic, just a few semi-trucks and an occasional car. She imagined one of those cars approaching. Perhaps it would slow down as it passed the lane leading to her house. Or maybe it would turn off its lights and then turn into the lane. Or pass the lane, stop a hundred yards down the road, and the driver would get out and quietly walk back to the house.

If it was Chad, she knew what he would do. First he would kill her and then murder her mom and dad.

She had talked to Dutton on the telephone the previous afternoon.

"Chad is still in L.A.," he assured her.

"Are you sure?"

"We're sure. We know where he is twenty-four/seven. I promise to call you if anything changes."

"When will this be over?"

"I'm not sure. Sometimes an investigation like this takes time."

"This is killing me. I can't sleep. I jump at the slightest noise. I'm afraid to be around people."

"We're working on it day and night. I'll call you the minute I know something."

It was near dawn when Kristen finally went back to the house and fell into an exhausted sleep.

That afternoon, a little before one, Kristen was still asleep when her mom came into her room. "Kristen, guess what? David is here! He just got home from his mission. Come say hello to him."

She crawled out of bed, threw on some clothes, and went to the bathroom. She ran a washcloth over her face and tried to rein in her out-of-control hair and quickly brushed her teeth. On her way out of the bathroom, she took a last look in the mirror and frowned. I look like I did when David used to call me Train Wreck.

Barefoot, she entered the living room. David, sporting a missionary haircut and wearing a white shirt and tie, immediately stood. He was grinning, but he looked nervous.

Kristen crossed the room and stood in front of him. After an awkward moment he held out his hand.

"We're going to shake hands, are we?" she asked, smiling.

He blushed. "For now." They shook hands.

"For now?" she asked. "What's coming later?"

He blushed even more. "Nothing."

"What a relief. Welcome back, Elder."

"You're . . ." he stammered.

"A late sleeper? Yes, it's true. I couldn't sleep last night."

"I didn't mean that."

"What did you mean?"

"You look great."

She shook her head and scowled. "You're easily impressed. I'm Train Wreck. Remember?"

"Not anymore," he said.

"Well, thanks. You look good."

Kristen's mother had stayed in the room. "Six more months and Zach will be home," she said.

"Yeah, I can't wait to see him," David said.

"I'm sure he feels the same way," Kristen's mom said.

"So, how was your mission?" Kristen asked.

He smiled. "Do you really want to know, or are you just being polite?"

"No. I really want to know."

The three of them sat down. As Kristen tried to act enthusiastic about what he was telling them, her mind was racing. *What will he think about me when Chad is arrested and I'm linked to him?* She flashed back to the things she had done in California and how easily she had given in to the temptations. She studied David's face as he talked about his experiences. *He seems so . . . clean, so . . . spiritual. Why did I let Chad sway me, when I knew it was wrong?* She didn't contribute much to the conversation as her mom and David visited.

After fifteen minutes or so, David said he needed to go. They shook hands again, and as he walked to his car, Kristen and her mom stood at the front door watching him.

"It was so nice of David to come by and see you, wasn't it?" her mom said.

"He didn't come to see me. He came to find out how Zach is doing."

"Maybe so, but his eyes lit up when you came into the room."

David backed his car around and pulled away.

"He just was surprised I've grown up, that's all." Kristen turned back into the house.

"Are you getting up now?" her mom asked.

"No."

"It's almost two o'clock."

"I couldn't sleep last night." She returned to her room and crawled back into bed.

Thursday, April 10

Like a caged lion, Chad paced back and forth in his apartment. Every few minutes he would look out the window to see if the grey Pontiac

Grand AM with a man inside was still parked across the street. The car had been there for two hours. Before that, there had been a cable repair truck parked in the apartment complex parking lot, again with a man inside. That had replaced a woman with a baby stroller who stood and talked with another woman. They talked for exactly two hours.

This much he knew: he and the rest of the Monkey Boys were under surveillance. Not that he'd picked it up just by being observant. One of his informants, a cop, had sent him an e-mail message looking like Spam, which they had previously agreed would tip him off that they were being watched.

The only unknown for Chad was how long they had been watched. *What do the cops know? What are they waiting for?*

He reasoned that the cops had not suspected them forever. If they had been on to the Monkey Boys, they would not have stood by and let them raid the last money house. They would have made an arrest on the spot.

Maybe they don't know anything. But if they don't know anything, why are they doing surveillance?

He could think of only one reason, and that was Kristen Boone. And the first thing he remembered when he thought of Kristen was the laptop he'd given her.

What an idiot I was, he thought. *Even though I deleted all my files, they can all be recovered. I knew that. What was I thinking? I've got to get that laptop back.*

I'll drive up to Idaho and pick it up. But if I do that, I'll be followed, and after I leave, some cop will ask her why I was there. And she'll tell him, and then they'll know. She's been nothing but trouble to me from the beginning.

If she'd stayed with me that night, then I could have used the video to blackmail her. A good Mormon girl like her would do anything, even lie to cops, to prevent something like that from becoming public.

Why did she leave that night after all the careful planning I'd done to make it happen? Who does she think she is anyway? Nobody messes with me that way.

I can't stay cooped up like this all the time. I know what we'll do. They want to tail us? Fine, they can. We'll keep them busy, going to clubs, eating out, going to the beach, having good clean fun. They'll run out of time and money before they ever catch us doing anything that is in any way suspicious.

Monday, April 14

When Dutton was told by his boss that the Monkey Boys investigation would now be a joint investigation, involving both NORSAT, from the sheriff's department, and an investigative branch of the Los Angeles Police Department, he asked, "Who will I be working with?"

"Morgan."

"Not Morgan," Dutton complained. "Anybody but Morgan."

"It will be Morgan, so get over it."

Dutton and Morgan had clashed before. They had huge philosophical differences over what law enforcement should be. Morgan felt his job was to get bad guys off the street, dead or alive. Dutton believed his job was to get them into the criminal justice system.

At their very first meeting, they had argued. "If it was up to me—" Morgan began.

"That's just it," Dutton said. "It's not up to you, and with any luck it never will be. We enforce the law. We're not a law unto ourselves. That's the way it has to be."

"You want to know what the trouble with you is?" Morgan asked. "You've never seen your partner killed by some low-life scumbag that, only a week before, had been arrested and then released by some bleeding-heart judge. You've never had to go tell his wife that her husband wouldn't be coming home. You didn't have to go to the funeral and see his two kids crying their hearts out for their daddy. Something like that changes the way you look at law enforcement and the animals we deal with. Your head is in the clouds, Dutton. That's what's wrong with you."

The one thing Dutton could not excuse was the way Morgan trained his men to make arrests.

Dutton's method was containment, cool-down, negotiation, and then arrest. And he had proved that it worked. NORSAT had a record of four years of arrests without a shot being fired on either side.

Morgan had a different approach. One car full of hardened criminals, four police cars, just like with Dutton's method. The car in front slows down and stops. One car comes to either the left or right side of the bad guys' car, but not both sides. Instead of a police car coming from behind and touching bumpers, it crashes into the suspects' car, sometimes hard enough to set off air bags.

The crucial difference is that one side of the car is not contained, so the suspects have a way to escape. It's what some officers called "the cone of death."

Being run into from behind kicks in the fight-or-flight instinct. The suspects decide to make a run for it. They exit the car, in some cases, with guns blazing. The cops stand behind their vehicles and shoot them all. In some cases they only wound the suspects, but in many cases, they kill them on the spot.

As Morgan liked to say privately, "They're bought and paid for." What he meant was, if the suspects make a run for it, if they fire their weapons, there's not a court in the land that will fault cops for using deadly force to prevent them from escaping. Under those circumstances, cops can kill them with no consequences.

"Dutton, have you looked around lately?" Morgan had asked him. "We're losing. On every side, we're losing. Unscrupulous defense attorneys, lenient judges who let guilty people off on technicalities, juries who feel sorry for these 'poor, misunderstood boys.' They think they need a hug. What they need is a nightstick up the side of the head. We're pampering criminals, and it isn't working. If you can't see that, I feel sorry for you."

Although neither could convince the other about an arrest strategy, they agreed that when it came time to arrest the Monkey Boys, whoever was on duty at the time would decide the way the arrest was conducted.

Friday, April 18

Dutton glanced at the Monkey Boys surveillance log. He shook his head and tossed the clipboard back on his cluttered desk and glanced up at Morgan. "We've spent thousands of dollars during the last few weeks, and for what? To watch the Monkey Boys taking their girls out to eat, and going to clubs, movies, and the beach. Our boys are on their best behavior," Dutton said. "They must know we're watching them."

"How about if we officially pull the plug, but set up a covert team, unknown to anyone, that will continue the investigation?" Morgan suggested.

Dutton's eyebrows raised. "That's actually a good idea."

Morgan smiled. "I have my moments."

The next day they pulled in the surveillance teams. They let it be known to their men that because of budget constraints and other more pressing cases, they were officially suspending the Monkey Boys investigation.

The next day, using undercover officers loaned to them from the gang units, Dutton and Morgan organized a small, secret task force that would continue working the Monkey Boys case. They used specially encrypted cell phones and vehicles that had never been used in any investigation, and in fact were registered to private individuals not connected to any law enforcement agency.

The test to determine if they were being successful was to see if Chad Nieteri would begin to act as if he were not being watched.

Thursday, April 24

Chad called Kristen with a request. "Hey, Kristen. How's it going up there in Idaho?"

He sounded friendly, but just hearing his voice gave Kristen chills. She needed to pretend nothing was wrong, but she was afraid her voice would give her away.

"Great. How's school?" she asked.

"Oh, same old, same old," he replied. "But I'm wondering. Do you still have my laptop?"

"Oh, sorry. I've been meaning to send it, but I haven't gotten around to it yet."

"Could you Fed-Ex it to me right away?" Chad asked.

"Yeah, sure, I'll send it today."

By that time, Chad's laptop had been to Washington, D.C., where FBI computer experts had retrieved the files that had been deleted. The laptop had been returned to Kristen in the same condition it had been in when Chad had given it to her.

The next day, Chad signed for the Fed-Ex package and shut the door to his apartment. He sat at his kitchen table, pulled the laptop out of the box, turned it on, and began to search for any clues that someone other than Kristen had used it. After an hour he was convinced nobody had tampered with it.

With that no longer a worry, he began to relax. A few days earlier, his informant had let him know that the police surveillance on him and his friends had been terminated.

This was coming just in time. He was running out of money. It was time for the Monkey Boys to get back in the game.

Tuesday, April 29, 9:30 p.m.

Morgan was in a bar watching a ball game on television and talking to a woman fifteen years younger, buying her drinks, trying to impress her by telling her about police work in L.A.

Morgan took a cell-phone call indicating that the Monkey Boys were at their storage units, suiting up to raid a money house. He got a big smile on his face.

"I'll be right there. Wait forty-five minutes and then call Dutton. Tell him not to worry and that I'll be in charge of the arrest."

They would wait until the Monkey Boys raided the money house, then pull them over as they fled. They'd catch them in their police gear and with the loot. Morgan was excited. It was a perfect setup. Because he was in charge, he'd order the officers under him to set up the cone-of-death confinement.

*   *   *

With Andy driving, the Monkey Boys pulled away from the crack house they had raided. They'd taken a huge amount of money from the dealers and were whooping it up as they drove along a four-lane surface street leading to the freeway.

"Oh, man," Mike said, "would you look at this?" He pulled a fistful of currency out of the canvas bag.

"Did you see that one guy?" Tyler said, "When we barged in, he looked like he was going to barf."

In their exuberance, they hadn't noticed, but an unmarked car had passed them and pulled into the same lane, about four car lengths ahead. A second car followed behind, but not close enough to cause any concern. And then a third car came up on their left as if it were passing but slowed to keep pace.

Suddenly the car in front slowed down. The car in back pulled up, and the car on their left pulled closer to them.

The car in front slammed on its brakes. Andy hit his brakes, but he couldn't stop fast enough and plowed into the rear of the car ahead. At the same moment, the car behind crashed into them. The drivers of the three unmarked vehicles jumped out of their cars and took up positions behind the car in back, guns drawn.

"This is the police! You're under arrest. Throw out your weapons and come out with your hands up!"

"Let's make a run for it!" Tyler shouted, throwing open the back door on the passengers' side and leaping from the car. From the front seat, Mike and Andy followed him, scrambling madly to get out of the car and run toward the side of the road. Only Chad stayed in the car, ducking down in the backseat and drawing his weapon.

As he ran, Tyler turned back and fired a shot at the police and was immediately gunned down, sprawling onto the grass parkway at the side of the road. Mike was next. He made it twenty feet before he tripped and fell to the ground. He rolled over onto his back, squirming backward and firing wildly toward the stalled cars. The police returned his fire, quickly putting an end to his resistance. Dodging as he ran, Andy darted between two houses, with two officers following him. After a few moments, three more shots rang out in the darkness.

In the confusion, Chad opened the back door on the driver's side of the car far enough to slip out undetected. Lying on his back, he squirmed under the vehicle next to the getaway car and came up on the far side. The driver's door was open and the engine still running.

With their attention on the other three gunmen, the police were surprised when Chad sped away, leaving three frustrated officers and three disabled cars in the road.

A few minutes later, Chad slowed down and turned off into a residential area. When he was within a mile of another of their storage units, he parked the car in the driveway of a house for sale, stashed his police gear in the trunk of the car, and began to walk.

Spotting a dog across the street, he called to it. It came and seemed content to walk with him. When he passed a small tree that had been staked, he cut the rope, attached it to the dog's collar, and continued walking.

He was a man taking his dog for a walk, and that made him of no interest to anyone searching for a desperate criminal.

He met a woman walking her dog. He smiled. "Nice night, isn't it?" he asked.

"Yes, it is. We need rain though."

"Wouldn't that be great?" he agreed.

He could hear sirens in the distance, but they didn't seem to be coming his way.

When he reached the storage facility, he removed the rope from the dog and let it go.

He undid the lock and opened the door. There was an older model, dark-colored car parked inside. Chad had bought it from an elderly woman just after her husband died. He had given her cash for the car and never switched plates, so as far as the state of California was concerned, the car belonged to the woman's deceased husband. There was no way it could be traced to him.

He opened the trunk to inspect its contents. He had thought of everything he'd need if he ever had to escape arrest—changes of clothing, food, water, guns, ammunition, police gear, and ten thousand dollars in cash.

A short time later, Chad was heading east on I-10.

He turned on the radio and listened to the breaking news about a deadly shooting that night in which three men had been killed while trying to escape arrest.

Chad couldn't believe it. With his adrenaline pumping, he hadn't considered what might have happened to his friends. There had been a lot of gunfire, but could they all really be dead? Those three guys had been his best friends. What had gone so wrong, so quickly? One minute they were all alive, the next minute they were gone. Shared experiences going clear back to when they were in grade school rushed through his mind, and he began to cry.

"I'm sorry, guys. I'm really sorry. I don't know what went wrong, but I'll find out. And when I do, it'll be payback time."

Driving had always helped him clear his mind.

His thoughts kept coming back to his old laptop. *I checked it out,* he thought. *Nothing had changed. It was exactly the way it had been when I gave it to Kristen.*

Exactly the same.

He paused.

Wait a minute. It shouldn't have been exactly the same. She said she was playing solitaire on it every day. But when you keep using the same software over and over, the icon for it appears on the most-often-used program list. But it wasn't there.

So she wasn't playing solitaire. And yet she said she was. So what else did she lie about?

He tried to stay in control. *The fact that she wasn't playing solitaire doesn't necessarily mean she turned my laptop over to the police. She might have just said that to make me feel like she was getting some use out of it.*

Maybe she's not responsible for all that's gone wrong. I just need to go talk to her. But if I find out she set me up, so help me, I'll kill her.

An hour later, he was on I-15 heading north.

He put the car on cruise control at five miles per hour under the speed limit so he wouldn't be picked up.

He felt better having a plan. If it turned out he had to kill Kristen, he'd do it and then slip across the Canadian border.

CHAPTER EIGHT

Wednesday, April 30, 3:00 A.M.

Exhausted and discouraged, Dutton pulled into the driveway of his house. He had been directing the manhunt for Chad Nieteri, but they hadn't come up with anything, even though they had every law enforcement agency in California and surrounding states looking for him.

Morgan had spent his time doing TV and newspaper interviews, enjoying the chance to make himself and his men look good.

Dutton was certain that if NORSAT had coordinated the arrest, nobody would have died, and the officers' lives would not have been endangered.

Whenever Dutton was discouraged by his job, he would always turn to a study of Moroni, chief captain over the Nephites. He sat at the kitchen table and began with Chapter 43 in Alma. He thought it might be somehow comforting to learn about a manhunt Moroni had once been involved in.

"But it came to pass, as soon as they had departed into the wilderness Moroni sent spies into the wilderness to watch their camp; and Moroni, also, knowing of the prophecies of Alma, sent certain men unto him, desiring him that he should inquire of the Lord whither the armies of the Nephites should go to defend themselves against the Lamanites."

Dutton thought, *Let's see. I don't have access to the prophet, so what can I do?*

He sat at the kitchen table and prayed for help in locating Nieteri, then got out a pad of paper and a pencil and wrote, "How is Chad Nieteri managing to escape arrest? Is he holed up somewhere, or is he on the move? And if he is on the move, where is he going?"

His wife entered the kitchen. "Long night?" she asked.

"Yeah."

"Well, you did your best. Now you need to sleep."

He nodded and looked at the questions he'd written.

"I mean now, cowboy," Laura said sternly. "The world's problems will still be there after you get some sleep."

He stood up, took one last look at the questions on the paper, and followed Laura to their room.

When he woke up the next morning, the house was quiet, and the room, even with the blinds shut, was filled with light. He looked at the clock. It was ten o'clock.

He threw on his favorite pair of pants and a T-shirt and went into the kitchen. After going to the front door and retrieving the newspaper, he grabbed a carton of milk, a box of cereal, and a bowl and spoon.

While he munched his cereal, he read the account of the attempted arrest of the Monkey Boys. *What's wrong?* he thought. *Morgan knowingly ignores recommended procedures for arrest, they kill three young men, and that makes his men heroes the next day? Officers killing the sons of other officers? Sure, that makes sense. And are these officers heroes to the mothers of the boys they killed? And if one of the officers had been shot, would Morgan still be a hero to that officer's family?*

Disgusted, he shoved the newspaper to the other side of the table and glanced at the second question he'd written the previous day. *Is he holed up somewhere, or is he on the move?*

At first, either possibility seemed equally likely. But then he thought back to the first time he met the four boys. It was at that first picnic, when he'd watched Chad taunt and ridicule one of his friends.

Dutton imagined that Chad liked to think of himself as being smarter than anyone in law enforcement. He would not let himself be caught hiding like some rat in a sewer. It would be a sweet victory for him to just get in a car and drive out of town.

He has only one means of transportation out of town. He can't book a flight or even take a bus or train. So that leaves driving. But how is it possible he could be driving when we can account for every car the Monkey Boys had in their possession? Could it be he's using a car we don't know about?

If he's driving, where will he go? He could head south. With enough money, he could find some local corrupt police chief in some out-of-the-way place, either in Mexico or some South American country, who might be persuaded to let him live there as long as he kept forking out the money.

If he's heading to Mexico, how will he get across the border? A fake I.D. won't help him. We've got his picture plastered at every border crossing. Would he hike twenty miles across a desert? No, he's too lazy for that. He likes things easy—he likes using his head, not his muscles, to get what he wants. I can't picture Chad walking twenty miles in the desert.

What about going north to Canada? Maybe, but what does he gain? If he can stay undetected in Canada, he can do the same in this country.

If he goes north, he'd have a chance to see Kristen.

For the second time in twelve hours, Dutton called Kristen's home. The first time had been right after Chad had escaped arrest. At that time he told her he expected they'd arrest him within a few hours.

Her mother answered.

"This is Dutton with the L.A. Sheriff's office."

"Yes, what news do you have for us?"

"We still haven't arrested Chad."

A long pause on the other end. "I see. Kristen told us you thought it would be any minute."

"Yes, I know. I'm sorry. Can I talk to Kristen?"

"Just a minute, please."

A short time later, Kristen came on the phone.

"Hello?"

"This is Dutton."

"My mom says you haven't got him yet."

106

"That's right. We've got hundreds of law enforcement personnel searching for him. It's just a matter of time." He cleared his throat. "There's just one thing."

"What's that?"

"I'm worried he might be coming your way."

Dutton could hear the conversation between Kristen and her mom. "What's wrong?" her mom asked.

"He thinks Chad might be coming here."

"He said they were about to arrest him. What happened?"

"He got away. They don't know where he is."

Her mother picked up the phone to talk to Dutton. "Why haven't you arrested Chad yet?"

"We're doing everything we can."

"This is not fair to my daughter. She hasn't done anything wrong."

"It's okay, Mom," Kristen said. She took the phone from her mother and told Dutton good-bye.

A short time later, Dutton called the Ashton Police Department and explained the situation to the man on duty.

"We'll do our best. I'll go by their place in the morning and also in the evening."

"I don't suppose there's any possibility you could assign an officer there night and day until we've arrested Nieteri," Dutton said.

The man chuckled. "We'll do what we can. We don't have a big California budget to work with up here. Besides, you don't even know for sure he's heading this way, do you?"

"No. If I find out he is, I'll get back to you."

"Yes, you do that, for sure."

Dutton hung up the phone and sat there in a stupor. He was exhausted from lack of sleep, depressed that the attempted arrest had gone so horribly wrong, and he felt helpless to protect Kristen if Chad was in fact on his way to see her.

I need to go to Idaho to protect Kristen, he thought.

*   *   *

At 11:30 A.M. at a rest stop on I-15 near Cedar City, Utah, Chad heard a noise, grabbed his gun, sat up and looked around. A car had just pulled next to him at the rest stop where he'd pulled off to sleep. A man in his sixties and his wife got out with their dog on a leash.

"Here we are, Muffin, do your thing," the woman said as the two of them followed their dog onto the lawn.

Chad placed the gun under a newspaper, so it wouldn't be seen, rubbed his hand across his chin, aware of the stubble. He needed to shave but didn't have a razor and didn't have the time to get one. He'd clean up after he'd taken care of Kristen.

He got out of his car and walked casually to the rest room.

The man and his dog were in the rest room. While Chad was washing his hands, the dog came over and sniffed at him.

"No, Muffin, leave him alone." The man pulled on the leash to get the dog away from Chad. "Sorry about that."

"No problem. In fact, I like dogs."

"Her name is Muffin."

"Good morning, Muffin," Chad said, crouching to pet the dog. Muffin licked his hand. Chad smiled weakly, stood up and washed his hands again.

"I see from your license plates you're from California, too. What part?" the man asked.

"L.A."

"We used to live there, but now that I'm retired, we live in Fernbrook. You know where that is?"

"No." Chad was not having much luck getting the electric hand dryer to work. It blew air when he pushed the button, but when he let go to rub his hands together, it turned off.

"You know where Poway is?" the man asked.

"Can't say I do." Chad gave up on the dryer, dried his hands on his shirt, and started out the door.

The man and Muffin followed him.

"Well, Poway is right next to San Diego. You've heard of San Diego, haven't you?" The man laughed at his own joke. "Fernbrook is very small, but my wife and I like it."

They were standing in back of Chad's car. The man's wife came out of the women's rest room and was heading their way.

"This young fellow is from Los Angeles."

"Really? What a coincidence!" the woman said.

"Yep, it is," the man said. "To think we'd have to both leave California to meet each other. I asked him if he knew where Fernbrook was, but he didn't."

The woman smiled. "Nobody ever knows where it is."

"I've got to go," Chad said. "It's been real nice meeting you both."

He was about to get in the car when the man started laughing. "Boy, you're in real trouble!"

Chad glanced at the newspaper on the passenger seat, wondering if he should go for his gun. "Trouble? What kind of trouble?"

"Look at your license plate."

"Why?"

"It's expired. Come here and I'll show you."

Chad walked to the back of the car.

"You see that little decal on the license plate? It should read 0-three, but yours reads 0-two. So it's been expired a long time. You must not drive this car much, right? Because if you did, you'd have been pulled over long ago."

"My niece had that happen to her a few years ago," the woman said. "I can see how it would happen. People these days are so busy and they get so much junk mail, it's hard to know what to open and what to throw away."

"Thanks for pointing that out. I'll take care of it right away."

"Well, you won't be taking care of it in Utah, that's for sure," the man said. "You'll have to go back to California. If I were you, I'd do most of my traveling at night. But, come to think of it, I guess that's what you've been doing anyway, right? You got something else you're hiding from us?" the man asked with a grin.

"No, not me, but thanks for noticing. I'd hate to get pulled over for something as simple as that." He started for his car.

"Do you want to say good-bye to Muffin before you leave?" the woman asked.

Chad forced himself to smile. "Well, of course." He went to the dog, knelt down, and rubbed the dog behind the ears. "Good-bye, Muffin, it's been great. I hope the lawn here in Utah was up to your standards."

Muffin licked his hand again.

"The lawn up to his standards! That's very funny! Isn't that funny, Dot?"

"It is! It's very funny!"

"Well, you take care, young fella. Oh, what's your name?"

"Steve Jackson," Chad said.

"Well, you take care, Steve."

The man and his wife waved as Chad pulled out of the parking lot. Chad wiped the dog's saliva from his hand on the seat cushion next to him.

"This is not a problem," he reassured himself as he pulled into the right lane. "Who notices license plates anyway? Nobody. As long as I stay on the road, nobody will ever notice. As long as I don't get pulled over for speeding, I'll be okay."

Half an hour later, he noticed in his rearview mirror a Utah Highway Patrol car. It was still a long way back, but rapidly closing the distance between them. It wasn't hard to imagine that when the officer got close enough, he might discover Chad's registration was expired. If that happened, he would pull Chad over. When the registration in the car didn't match his I.D., the officer might radio in for them to run a check on his name. That's all it would take.

Chad increased his speed to match the car behind him, but doing that put him over the speed limit. *What if he pulls me over for speeding? What then?*

The highway patrolman increased his speed. Chad panicked. *If I go any faster, I will be pulled over.*

A sign indicated a rest stop in one mile. He sighed. "Just one more mile and then this will be over." He turned on his turn signal.

The car behind him also began to signal.

Chad lifted the newspaper and reached for his gun and set it on the seat next to his hip.

A minute later he pulled into the rest stop. The highway patrol car pulled in next to him.

Chad got out and opened the trunk of his car, as if he were looking for something. The officer stepped out of his car, stretched, and walked to the rest room.

Chad waited a minute, closed the trunk, got back into his car, and drove away.

He had a litany of swear words he used when he was under stress. He went through them over and over until finally he felt in control again. "I'm not going through this again. I need new plates."

*   *   *

When Dutton had a problem he couldn't solve, he liked to write down a list of all the possible solutions. It helped him organize his thoughts. He was just starting to do that a little before two in the afternoon when Morgan entered his office and closed the door. "What happened?" Dutton asked. "Run out of media to give interviews to?"

Morgan chuckled. "You're not jealous, are you?"

"No, that's not what I am."

"Well, good. This is your victory too. Aren't you going to congratulate us?"

"For what, gunning down three people and endangering your men? Or should I congratulate you on Nieteri escaping your botched arrest? Who knows, if things go your way, you might kill him yet. And then you can meet and greet the media all over again."

"Why are you even in law enforcement, Dutton? Why don't you go join some group that feels that any kind of police brutality is bad?"

"It's obvious you don't feel that way."

"No—as they say, the end justifies the means."

"Did you come in here for a specific reason or just to gloat?" Dutton asked.

"I came to tell you we've got a lead on Nieteri. I expect we'll be bringing him in any moment."

"Where do you think he is?"

"We talked to one of the girls who used to hang around with the Monkey Boys—a gal named Summer Gillespie. They went out on a yacht once, and Chad said it was his. She thinks he's on that boat, on his way to Mexico. We've contacted the Coast Guard and the Mexican authorities."

"Are you going to kill him, too?"

"We'll surround him and order him to throw down his guns. If he doesn't comply, I suppose he could get hurt."

"I think he's heading north."

Morgan laughed. "Why would he do that?"

"To go to Idaho and kill Kristen Boone."

"You can think what you want, but we're the ones who are going to bring him in today, dead or alive."

"I'm thinking of going to Idaho to protect her."

"Based on what?"

"Right now I don't have anything." Dutton stood up to escort Morgan to the door. "Good luck in Mexico."

"You have no reason to think he's going to Idaho. Get something to justify that conclusion. You'll look like a fool if we pick him up in Mexico while you're wasting taxpayers' money in Idaho."

Dutton nodded. "All right, I'll see what I can find."

As soon as Morgan left, Dutton phoned Kristen again.

"Have you caught him yet?" she asked.

"Not yet, but we're working on it. I need to ask you a question. Did Chad always drive the same car?"

"Most of the time, but once he gave me a ride in a car that he'd just bought."

"So did he sell the old car?" Dutton asked.

"No, I just saw the new car once, and from then on, he drove his old car."

"Did he ever tell you what happened to the new car?" Dutton asked.

"No, not really. I asked him once, and he told me he couldn't afford to keep it, so he got rid of it."

"All right, thanks. That's all I need. I'll keep you posted."

Dutton drove to Chad's apartment where a team of investigators was going through the place.

"What have you got?" Dutton asked the officer in charge.

"We found a receipt for two storage units. I assumed you'd want us to check it out, so I've asked for a warrant. As soon as we get it, Liu and Ostler will search the units. I'm hoping to get that done this afternoon."

"Good. What else?"

"Not much. Oh, Nieteri had a concealed video recording system in his living room and bedroom, and we found some spicy viewing of the girls he brought to his place. He labeled each recorded video by date. We haven't looked at everything yet."

Dutton hated to ask but felt as though he had to. "Are there any videos of him with Kristen Boone?"

"Just one. They make out for a while, but then they get into an argument and she walks out."

Dutton was relieved to hear that.

Two hours later, Dutton pulled up to the two unlocked storage units where officers were doing an inventory. His mouth dropped open as he approached the units. Except for the location, the shelves and police equipment looked like they might have come from any metropolitan police station.

"Welcome to NORSAT West," one of his men said, shaking his head.

"Give me a tour," Dutton said.

They slowly went through the shelves. "Look at this stuff!" the officer said. "They've got everything we've got—guns, raid equipment, Sam Brownes, Flash Bangs, smoke grenades, surveillance cameras, two-way radios, the works."

The two of them talked for a few minutes. When Dutton turned, he spotted a thin, nervous-looking man sitting in his car smoking a cigarette.

"Who's that?" he asked.

"The manager of the storage facility. He's afraid we're going to take him to jail."

"I'll go talk to him."

The man had his car running and the air conditioning on. Dutton knocked on the driver's side window.

The man rolled the window down a few inches. "Yes?"

"My name is Dutton. I work with the L.A. County Sheriff's office. I have a few questions I'd like to ask you."

The man turned off the engine and got out of the car.

"What's your name?" Dutton asked.

"Emerson Fletcher. I just want to say that I have no way of knowing what people store in their units."

"No, of course you don't," Dutton said.

"These were the ones who were shot by the police last night, weren't they?"

"Yes, they were."

"I saw it on TV this morning," Mr. Fletcher said. "Nice-looking boys."

Dutton nodded.

"One is still on the loose, is that right?"

"Right."

"When they showed his picture on TV, I recognized him. Nieteri is his name. He was the one who rented the units."

Dutton showed him the receipt for the units. "I notice he paid for one whole year. Is that common?"

Mr. Fletcher shook his head. "Most people pay month to month." He looked puzzled. "Is that important?"

"I'm interested in finding out if they rented other storage units. So if he paid yearly, but most people pay once a month, then we can contact other places and ask for a list of their customers who pay once a year."

"Oh, I see." He paused. "Actually, he paid for three units."

"He did? Where's the other one?"

"At another of our locations."

"I would really like to see what is in that unit. Could I follow you there?" Dutton asked.

Thirty minutes later, Fletcher unlocked a storage unit and glanced over at Dutton. "You're stronger than me. You open it up."

Dutton lifted the overhead door. The only thing in the unit was a five-year-old Mercury Sable.

"Some folks store their antique cars, but this is not antique," Fletcher said.

"No, it sure isn't."

"Then why store it?" Fletcher asked.

"I think I know the reason. If you passed this car, would you pay any particular attention to it?"

"No, sir, I wouldn't. It's just another car."

"That's the reason to have it. Mr. Fletcher, I need to find out what's inside the car."

"I can't give you permission to do that."

"I know you can't. I'm not asking for permission. All I need you to do is go back to your car and wait for me. I'll be a few minutes. And then, and this is the last thing I'll ask of you, I'd like you to wait for some other officers who will do a more complete investigation of the car."

Dutton used a punch and a hammer to shatter the front passenger window.

Once inside the car he went through the backseat to get to the trunk. He found ten thousand dollars in cash, some canned goods, a police raid jacket, and a siren and emergency light that can be plunked on a car during a chase.

He called Delilah, his secretary. "I want you to call Becker and Deltoro and have them come in."

"They work nights."

"Get them in there now. I want them to contact every storage facility in a twenty-mile radius and get a list of units that are paid for once a year with cash. And then I want them to get warrants and get them opened up. If they find a car, I want to know about it."

"Okay, I'll get them on it."

"Thanks. They can contact me on my cell phone. If they can't reach me, have them leave a message. Oh, and I need you to book me the next flight for Idaho Falls."

4:00 p.m.; Nephi, Utah

Chad wiped the sweat from his forehead, checked the address on the house with one he'd circled on a shopper's guide, and started toward the house.

It was a small, white frame house, and its front yard was littered with toys and bikes.

He rang the doorbell. A tired looking woman in her early forties came to the door.

"I'm the one who called about the car," Chad said.

"Oh, yes." She looked around. "Did you walk?"

"I did, actually."

"You should've told me you were on foot. I could have given you a ride."

"Oh, that's okay. I enjoyed the walk."

"Can I get you some water?"

"No, thanks. I would like to see the car though."

A minute later he was looking at a ten-year-old Honda Accord.

"What can you tell me about it?" Chad asked.

"Well, not too much. My husband will be home in a couple of hours, if you want to wait. He knows more about the car than I do. It belonged to our son. He's serving a mission now. My son didn't have any problems with it. At least not any that I know of."

A girl stuck her head out the back door. "Mommy, Melissa just threw up again."

"I'll be right there."

"It's on the living room floor."

The woman turned to Chad. "I'm sorry. Things are a little crazy here right now. Can you come back later and talk to my husband?"

"You know what? This is just what I'm looking for. I'd like to buy it."

"Without even driving it?"

"I'll take your word. How about I just pay you and be on my way?"

"Well, I need to take care of my daughter first."

"I'll wait."

"Would you like to come in?"

"I think I'll wait out here if that's all right."

"Of course. I'll go get the title."

Chad waited five minutes, but the woman didn't come out. Worried she might be calling the police or her husband, he stepped onto the porch.

He could hear the woman through the screen door. "Not now, Sweetheart. Mommy's looking for something."

"How are you coming in there?" Chad called.

"I know it's here somewhere."

"Is there anything I can do to help?" he asked.

"Well, actually, there is. Could you get my daughter some 7-Up and soda crackers? The soda's in the fridge, and the crackers are in the cupboard next to the stove."

Why me? Chad thought. "Okay, I'm coming in."

As he entered the house, the first thing that caught his attention was a wedding picture on the wall, apparently of the woman and her husband. He was struck by how much the young woman in the photo resembled Kristen.

A little girl in her pajamas was on the couch watching TV.

"Are you the sick one?" he asked.

She made a pouty face and nodded. "Who are you?"

"I'm here to help you get better." He walked into the kitchen.

A minute later he returned with an ice-filled glass of 7-Up and a small plate of crackers. He set everything on a table next to the couch and then sat down on the opposite side of the room from the girl. He didn't want to get whatever she had.

A few minutes later the woman returned with the title. "Did you thank the nice man for bringing you a drink and crackers?" she asked her daughter.

"Thank you," the girl said.

The woman sat down next to her daughter. "Okay, I found the title. Now what do we do?"

"I give you the money. You sign the title, and then I sign it, and then you give me the keys and I drive away. That's all there is to it."

She seemed surprised. "You brought the money with you?"

"I did." He pulled a roll of bills out of his pocket and then counted it for her and placed it on the coffee table in front of her.

She stared at the money and laughed. "What did you do, rob a bank?"

He forced a grin. "No, my life isn't that exciting. A while ago, I had some problems with credit cards and checking accounts. So now I do everything on a strictly cash basis. I know it's risky to be carrying so much cash, but so far it's worked out for me. And I'm completely debt-free now."

"Good for you. I wish we were. Well, okay, just show me where to sign."

He studied the title and then handed it to her. "Right here. Oh, and you're supposed to write in the asking price . . . right here."

She did as directed and then handed him the title.

"I'll need some keys, too," Chad said.

"Oh, of course, let me get them. I think we have two sets."

The woman left the room.

"What's your name?" the little girl asked him.

"Steve," he replied. "What's yours?"

"Melissa."

He glanced at his watch. *C'mon, I don't have all day.*

The woman called out from the kitchen. "I thought they were right here in this drawer."

"Are you a daddy?" the girl asked.

"Not that I know of."

She laughed. "If you're a daddy, you know it."

"Not always."

"You should be a daddy."

He started pacing the floor. *Maybe some day. If I ever get out of here, that is.*

"I found them!" the woman called out from the kitchen. She hurried in and handed him the keys. "I'm sorry it took so long. Our house isn't always this chaotic." She laughed. "Sometimes it's even worse."

"Hey, no problem."

He glanced at Melissa. "Hang in there, kid," he said. And then he turned to the woman. "Well, I have to go. Thanks again."

Chad only needed the Honda for the plates. But, because he didn't want the woman seeing it abandoned the next day, he drove it to a trailhead for the Mount Nebo Wilderness area, made sure nobody was around, removed the plates, and tucked them between the pages of a newspaper and hitchhiked back to town.

A short time later, he put the Utah plates on his car, and then got back on I-15 heading north.

My worries are over, he thought. *And if I find out Kristen has double-crossed me, her worries are about to begin.*

*   *   *

Bishop Loren Brower made his living raising seed potatoes. Apparently business was good because he had one of the nicest houses in the county.

Kristen knocked on the door. It was two-thirty in the afternoon.

"Kristen, what a surprise! Come in," Sister Brower said.

Kristen stepped inside.

"Please sit down. Would you like something to drink? I've got Sprite, orange juice, and cranberry juice."

Kristen sat down. "Actually, I was hoping I could talk to the bishop."

"Well, he's out on the tractor right now. Let me give him a call."

Kristen stood up. "You know what? This was a bad idea. I shouldn't have come out here. It can wait until Sunday. I'll just go now."

"No, it's okay. He needs a break anyway. Once he starts working, he doesn't know when to quit. I don't think he's even had lunch yet. Let me call him."

"It's not that important."

"Oh, it must be a little important, or you'd have never come out here." She grabbed her phone and punched in the number. "Loren, Kristen Boone is here. She would like to talk to you. Are you at a place where you can take a break? . . . All right. I'll tell her."

She laid the phone down and sat down across from Kristen. "He'll be here in a few minutes."

"Thank you," Kristen said.

"You're quite welcome. How is your family?"

"We're fine."

"What do you hear from Zach?"

"He's doing good. He's a zone leader now," Kristen said.

"That's not surprising. Let's see. You were in California going to school, weren't you?"

"Yes. I was at UCLA."

"So, you're home on a break, is that right?"

"Yes."

"Well, we're happy to have you with us again." She stood up. "I need to make a sandwich for my husband. You want to come in the kitchen? That way we can talk."

Kristen smiled faintly. "Would it be okay if I just stayed here?"

"Yes, of course." She stood up. "Well, if you need anything, just let me know."

"I will."

With Sister Brower gone, the need for forcing a smile was gone. Kristen sat with her hands folded in her lap and her head down.

Bishop Brower had been her bishop since she was fourteen years old. She had been the Mia Maid class president. Later she had served as the Laurel class president. She met with him often. He had once called her his shining star. She didn't feel much like that now.

My coming here was a big mistake. What was I thinking? she thought.

Fifteen minutes later Bishop Brower came into the house through the back door. Kristen could hear his booming voice. "It's a little warm out there today."

"Really? What does that mean, Loren?" Sister Brower teased. "That you had to put the air conditioning on a higher setting? Poor baby. I feel so sorry for you."

He laughed. "You got me there, Babe. So where's Kristen?"

"In the living room."

Bishop Brower was a big man with work-hardened hands and a hearty voice. During sacrament meeting, when he laughed, it could be heard throughout the building. Ward members teased him about it, but the truth was, his good nature put people at ease.

He came in the living room and shook her hand. "Kristen, it's so good to see you! What brings you out our way?"

"I really need to talk to you."

He nodded. "Sure, no problem. Let me go change my clothes."

"You don't have to do that."

"Are you coming to see me because I'm your bishop?"

"Yes."

He nodded. "Then I need to change. Excuse me. I'll be right back. Do you need anything? Something to drink?"

"No, thanks."

"I'll be right back, then," he said.

"I'm sorry to be putting you to so much trouble," she said.

"Don't you worry about that. Not one bit. Now, please excuse me."

A few minutes later he returned, wearing the suit and white shirt and tie he wore every Sunday. He brought in a dining room chair and set it down in front of her. "You know what? I haven't acted as a bishop all day. Would you mind if we had a prayer to help get me in the right spirit?"

"That would be good."

"If you want, I can offer the prayer," he said.

In his prayer he thanked Heavenly Father for His great plan of happiness and for the atonement of Jesus Christ. He asked a blessing for Kristen, that she would feel comfortable talking to him, and that he would be inspired to know what to say.

After the prayer, he said, "Now, what can I do for you?"

Kristen felt as though she might burst into tears, and she was wringing her hands.

"You look a little troubled, Kristen. Is there something you wish to tell me?"

Kristen glanced toward the kitchen.

The bishop noticed and said, "Sister Brower is in her sewing room. You don't have to worry about being overheard."

Kristen took a deep breath, then said quietly, "Bishop, I've made some mistakes that I need to get cleared up."

"What kind of mistakes?"

"I met a guy in California. His name is Chad. He was in one of my classes. Or at least he said he was. It was always fun to be with him. I don't know what happened. I guess I wanted to fit in."

Kristen shook her head. "The thing that surprises me is how easily I was willing to give up things I'd been taught all my life. I mean, the first time I was with Chad and his friends, I started drinking and I nearly got a . . . tattoo."

He smiled. "A tattoo? I can't imagine you with a tattoo."

"Everyone was getting one, but when it was my turn I chickened out. And the next day I skipped church because I felt guilty about drinking and, also, because I stayed up too late watching movies because I thought I was about to become a big movie star, and that I needed to learn how to do it."

She covered her face with her hands and rubbed her eyes. "That was the first time I was with Chad and his friends. I should have known that it wasn't going in the right direction. I should have quit seeing him then."

"But you didn't?"

"No. One time we'd gone out with his friends, and we'd all agreed to go to Chad's apartment and watch a movie. Except they never showed up. We started kissing. I knew it wasn't right for me to be alone with him in his apartment, but he kept telling me he was sure they'd be coming any minute. I knew what we were doing wasn't right, but I didn't do anything to stop him. But when he asked me to go with him to his bedroom, I freaked out. I got up and told him I couldn't stay there. He got really mad at me and started yelling at me. He told me I owed him for spending so much money on me. Well, I left right away and took a taxi back to my apartment."

"Good for you," the bishop said. "I'm proud of you for getting out of a bad situation."

With tears in her eyes, she shook her head. "Don't be proud of me, Bishop. That night when I first walked into his apartment, I had a strong prompting to leave. It was so clear to me that I needed to get out of there right away. But I didn't. That's what bothers me the most. What good are promptings if I don't heed them?"

"This is something that all of us struggle with. It takes humility to be receptive to the influence of the Holy Ghost. I know I've talked myself out of promptings I've received." He paused. "Was that the last time you saw Chad—was that his name?"

"Yes." She shook her head. "No. I wish it had been, but, no, it wasn't. A few days later he came and apologized. When he's in a good mood, it's very hard, at least for me, to turn him away. I guess I'd still be seeing him now . . . but Chad saw me walking with Jonathan. He's a friend of mine from my institute class." She paused. "I'm pretty sure Chad had some friends of his beat Jonathan up."

"Do you know that for sure?" the bishop asked.

"Not for sure, but Jonathan told me he saw Chad in his car watching him get beat up. I've seen Chad when he's angry, and it's not hard for me to believe he would do that."

"Sounds like this guy is bad news."

"It gets worse."

"It does?"

"Chad is wanted by the police."

"What for?"

"He and his friends impersonated cops and robbed drug dealers. When the police tried to arrest them, they shot and killed three of Chad's friends, but Chad escaped. He's on the loose. One of the policemen told me that Chad might come up here to get even with me."

"Get even with you for what?"

"Chad gave me his old laptop. When the policeman from Los Angeles came to talk to me about Chad, I let him have the laptop. I guess they found enough evidence on it to arrest him. If Chad figures that out, he may come up here to kill me."

"If you feel you and your family are in danger, you're welcome to stay here with us."

"We're talking about going to stay at my grandparents' place in Squirrel. It will all work out. Anyway, that's why I had to see you today instead of Sunday." With tears in her eyes, she looked away. "Because I'm not sure I'll be alive Sunday . . . and I wanted to get this cleared up before it's too late." She stood up. "I'd better go."

Bishop Brower also stood. "Have you had a priesthood blessing?"

"No."

"Please go home and ask your dad to give you one."

She nodded. "That's a good idea."

"I'm serious about your family staying here. Or whatever you need.

We can have some of the men from the ward watch your house twenty-four hours a day."

Kristen smiled sadly. "You're going to have the high priests staying up all night? They can't even stay awake during church."

He smiled and held on to her hand. "I'll call your dad and see what he'd like us to do. And I'll put your name on the prayer roll at the temple."

"Thank you, Bishop. I'm sorry to have taken you away from your work."

"I'm very glad you came. Call me anytime, day or night."

"I will. Bishop, can I take the sacrament on Sunday?"

"Is there anything else that you haven't told me?"

Kristen shook her head. "No."

"Then I think you should take the sacrament. That's what it's for—to help us repent of our mistakes. And from what you've told me, that's what you've done. Made some foolish choices."

"Thank you, Bishop."

He called for his wife.

"Yes?" she said, coming into the room.

"Please give this girl a big hug for me, will you?"

"My pleasure."

A short time later, as she pulled away from the bishop's house onto the highway, Kristen felt a sense of comfort and peace.

CHAPTER NINE

"You called my name?" Dutton asked the Delta agent, a few minutes before the flight to Salt Lake City was scheduled to leave.

"Yes, Officer Dutton. It looks like we will have room for you after all."

"Thanks. I appreciate your help."

Dutton received his seat assignment, grabbed his cell phone, and made a call.

Kristen answered it. "Yes?"

"Kristen, this is Dutton. Look, I don't have much time. We have reason to believe now that Chad has left L.A. by car. We don't know where he's going, but just in case he's heading your way, I'm coming up. Is there someplace you and your family can go that Chad won't know about?"

"We could stay at my grandparents' place. They live about thirty miles away. It's in the middle of nowhere. When will you get here?"

"I should definitely be there sometime tonight. I'll call later and get directions."

"Do you know yet if I'll have to testify at the trial?"

"I'm not sure."

"Chad and I were just good friends, that's all."

"I know. We have confirmation of that."

"How do you know?"

"Chad had a hidden camera and a video recording system in his apartment. Whenever he had a girl over, he recorded everything that happened in the living room . . . and in the bedroom."

"What? I can't believe it! That is so disgusting! Why would he do that? Oh, wait, don't tell me! I know why! So he could show it to his idiot friends, right? What a pervert! How could I have been so stupid to get involved with him!"

Dutton heard his flight being called. "Look, I've got to board my flight now. I'll call you from Idaho Falls."

He took two steps and then heard a voice. "Dutton! Wait!"

Dutton turned around to see Joseph DeSoto running toward him. DeSoto was one of the executive assistants to the sheriff. "We've got to talk," he wheezed, trying to catch his breath.

"I need to board my flight."

"Take a later flight. This is important. It's about the report you sent us dealing with the Vikings."

Dutton had the ticket agent book him for the next flight.

They ended up at a coffee shop. DeSoto, bald and round like a pear, ordered a cappuccino and two large muffins. Dutton settled for his usual glass of milk and a cookie.

"Let me tell you what's been going on lately," DeSoto said. "I know you've been preoccupied with the Monkey Boys case. Oh, by the way, congratulations for . . . apprehending three of the gang."

"We didn't apprehend them; we shot them dead. And don't thank me, thank Morgan."

"Whatever," DeSoto said with a shrug. "Anyway, five days ago a guy named Alex Sanchez, a county employee, was having a backyard birthday party for his daughter. I guess they had a lot of relatives there, and maybe they were a little noisy because some neighbor called in and complained. Four officers from the Lynwood Station responded. Somehow they mistook the event as being gang related. When they approached the house with guns drawn, Mr. Sanchez told them he was having a private party and asked them to leave."

DeSoto continued. "They grabbed Sanchez and dragged him to the car, drove to a utility trailer in the back of the Lynwood Station and beat him severely. When they were done with him, they returned to his house, dumped him onto the lawn, and drove away." DeSoto took a big bite of his muffin.

"I tried to warn you guys," Dutton said.

With his mouth full, DeSoto continued. "Sanchez is still in the hospital. Today we were contacted by an attorney representing Sanchez. It looks like this may end up being a multimillion-dollar lawsuit against us. Naturally we're concerned."

"Concerned? What concerns you the most, DeSoto? That an innocent man was nearly killed by rogue cops, or that it might be embarrassing to the department?"

"I'm as interested in making things better at the Lynwood Station as you are, but for the good of the department, we need to be very careful what we say and do from now on. That's why they sent me."

"Well?"

"First of all, I've been asked to thank you for sending us a written report about the Vikings. And of course we want to shut them down." He hesitated. "There's just one thing. We need to wait until after the Sanchez case is settled. It would be like writing a blank check if Sanchez's attorney learned how bad things are at the Lynwood Station. Especially if it were found out that you sent a report to us about the Vikings and we just sat on it. Information like that could dramatically hurt our chances in court."

"Maybe you should have thought about that when you received my report," Dutton said.

"Hindsight is always twenty-twenty, isn't it? Look, Dutton, it does no good talking about what we should have done. All we can do is try to do better in the future. I'm sure I don't have to tell you how severe it would be for us to be slapped with a multimillion-dollar settlement. So I'm wondering if you and I can come to some sort of an agreement."

"What would that agreement be?"

"Everyone agrees to keep quiet about your report. After the Sanchez suit is settled, we move ahead with purging the Vikings from the Lynwood Station, or any other station where they may exist."

"And how long will it be before the lawsuit is settled?" Dutton asked.

"That's hard to say. Two or three years is my guess."

"So immediately after the case is settled, you'll go in and clean out the Vikings from the Lynwood Station?" Dutton asked.

"Well, not right after, of course. We'd probably want to wait a year for the dust to settle."

Dutton stood up. "So, in four years you'll do the right thing? Listen to me! What happened to Sanchez is going on all the time at the Lynwood Station! What is wrong with you people to even suggest waiting?" He stood up and walked out.

DeSoto grabbed his remaining muffin and ran to catch up. "For crying out loud, we're on the same side, Dutton, and right now we need your cooperation."

"I can't go along with something that is so blatantly wrong," Dutton said, walking faster.

DeSoto gave up trying to keep up. "Dutton!"

Dutton stopped and turned around. "What?"

"I thought you enjoyed being NORSAT commander."

Dutton slowly walked back to him. "Is that a threat?"

DeSoto shrugged. "It's just reality, Dutton. We need people at the top who will work *with* us, not against us. We need loyalty."

"Loyalty to what? When I was sworn in as an officer, I took an oath that I would defend the Constitution of the United States as well as the Constitution of the State of California. I don't recall promising I'd go along with every morally bankrupt directive coming down from the top."

DeSoto lowered his voice. "I know you're angry, and that's okay. You should be. But let me tell you something. It's not just us you need to worry about. If the Vikings hear about your report, they may take things into their own hands."

"How would they hear about my report? Who would tell them? You?

I haven't talked to anyone about the report. Only you people have it. So who would tell them?"

"I don't know," DeSoto said.

"Are you saying that unless I cooperate, someone in your office might leak my report to the Vikings?"

"I am not saying that. It's just that for all we know, the Vikings could have someone working at headquarters. So if I were you, I would think very carefully about this. We'll talk when you get back."

"Fine. We can talk all you want, but I'm not going along with this." Dutton stared at DeSoto and shook his head.

"What?" DeSoto asked.

"How can you stand going to work every day?" Dutton asked.

"It's not always this bad."

"Good-bye, DeSoto."

*   *   *

After DeSoto left, Dutton had plenty of time on his hands until his flight left. He called Kristen and told her he would be later than he'd originally said.

And then he called Delilah. "What have you found out?" he asked.

"We've located two more cars that Nieteri had stored. They were spread out across town. Every one of them is a low-profile car. Oh, and each one was bought from a private owner. We've talked to three of the owners, and in every case, Nieteri paid cash. He only bought cars if the owner had the title. He would take the title, promising to register it under his name. But he never did. The car is still registered under the original owner's name. So he's off the hook."

"Clever."

"But there's one drawback. He can't get new tags. When the state mailed out the renewal notice to the original owners, one of them mailed it back, saying they'd already sold the car."

"See if you can find the license number for the car that Chad is driving."

"We're working on it. I'll get back to you as soon as we find it."

"Thanks."

Dutton sat and waited, wondering where Chad Nieteri was and what he was doing.

*   *   *

Chad looked at his watch. 8:30 P.M. He was in Idaho Falls. He had just turned off I-15 onto Highway 20 and was less than an hour away from Ashton.

He tried to picture what it would be like, seeing Kristen again. There had been times on the road when all he wanted to do was kill her, when he was convinced that the reason his friends were dead was that she'd cooperated with the cops. At other times he realized he didn't really have any proof of that.

Am I going to kill her just because she lied about playing solitaire? That doesn't make sense. It's more likely she didn't use the laptop at all, but didn't want to disappoint me, so she made up the story about playing solitaire.

We got along so well, at least most of the time. It's true she didn't put out for me, but if we'd continued seeing each other, it would've happened sooner or later. Besides, I like a good challenge.

I'll find a time to talk to her, just the two of us. If I find out she didn't betray me, then I'll talk her into coming with me to Canada. It could be good, just the two of us. Of course she couldn't ever contact her family again. I'm not sure she'd go along with that, but maybe she would.

He gritted his teeth. *There's always a chance I'll end up killing her. Either I'll find out she ratted me out, or she won't want to come with me. Either way I'll have to kill her. I can't have the cops knowing where I am.*

A few miles past Idaho Falls, he noticed a state police car pulling in behind him. Chad checked his speedometer. He was going exactly the speed limit.

He slowed down, hoping the car would pass, but it didn't.

I've got to exit, he thought.

He took the next exit. The state police car followed him.

He noticed a sign for a business called The Loft. It was surrounded with cars. He pulled in and parked. The car following him pulled in and stopped.

Chad got out of the car and walked into the building. At first he thought it was a restaurant, but then he noticed that the couple in front of him had a present in their hand. They were talking to a couple in front of them. "How do you know Josh and Emma?" one of the women asked.

"Josh played basketball for me at Madison High School."

"Wait a minute! You're Coach Lewis! Madison took state Josh's senior year, right?"

Chad quickly glanced back. The state police officer was standing in line, two or three people back. But what made Chad very happy was that the officer had a present in his hand.

Chad let out a sigh of relief and smiled to himself. *I'll be okay. All I have to do is go through the reception line, shake a few hands, and then leave.*

As soon as the line moved into the reception room, Chad couldn't keep his eyes off the bride. She was a knockout in her white wedding gown—tall and blond and shapely—and seemed to be happier than anyone Chad had ever seen. And she was hugging nearly everyone in line.

If I'm going to get a hug, I need an identity. Who am I? And which of the two do I know?

The first people in the reception line were the father and mother of the bride. Looking uncomfortable in his tuxedo, the man looked at Chad questioningly. Chad extended his hand and said, "I'm Donny. Josh and I were in school together."

"Well, thanks for coming. Rita, this is Donny, one of Josh's school buddies."

His wife smiled. She was short and plump and had on a lot of makeup and a dress that was a little too tight. She extended her hand, giving off a whiff of some kind of strong perfume. "Oh, nice to meet you, Donny. We're Emma's parents, the Websters."

Chad apologized for the casual way he was dressed and that he hadn't had time to shave. "I just drove in. I was worried I wouldn't make it on time."

"Oh, we're just glad you made the effort," Mrs. Webster gushed, giving off another blast of perfume, then turned to the people in line behind Chad.

Next in line were the bride and groom. The groom was still preoccupied with talking to his old coach.

Chad reached for the bride and gave her a hug. "Emma, I've heard so much about you!" He kissed her on the cheek. "You're beautiful."

"Thank you."

"No, thank *you*. I think Josh is the luckiest guy in the world."

Smiling, Emma turned her attention to the person behind Chad, a matronly woman wearing an outdated, flowered dress. "Oh, my gosh, Aunt Flo!" she squealed. "I can't believe you came all the way from Alaska!"

With both Emma and Josh deep in conversation, Chad studied Josh. He was clean-shaven, tall, and grinning self-consciously as he pumped his old coach's hand. *We're about the same age,* Chad thought. *I could be him.*

He turned his attention back to Emma. She seemed to be radiantly happy as she described for her aunt how she had met Josh while working at a lodge in Yellowstone Park.

Is this what it would be like if Kristen and I got married? Starting life out together, full of hope for the future? It could still happen. There's no reason I have to kill her. If she comes with me to Canada, we could take on new identities and eventually get married. We might even have kids.

Glancing at Emma again, he thought, *She's a babe. I should have kissed her on the lips. She wouldn't have minded. I missed my chance. Why am I so noble all the time?*

Josh and the coach had one more bear hug, and then Josh turned to Chad. Emma was still talking to her aunt.

He shook Josh's hand. "I'm a friend of Emma's," he said. "Congratulations. You're a lucky man." And then he moved quickly down the line, shaking hands with Josh's parents and the six identically dressed, giggling bridesmaids, who had all taken off their shoes.

On his way out, Chad was relieved that the police officer had paid no attention to him.

Outside, he decided to switch license plates with another car. Since he had Utah plates, he looked for cars with Utah plates. He found one that was parked in a darkened corner of the lot.

It took him ten minutes to make the switch, and then he continued on his way.

It was so dark he wasn't too worried that the driver of the other car would come out and notice his plates had been switched. The driver might not realize for several days that the switch had taken place. By that time Chad would be in Canada.

I'm in good shape, he thought. *Now all I have to do is go talk to Kristen. I hope she'll go with me to Canada.* He tried to visualize Kristen's face. It had been several weeks since he had seen her, and in his mind her features were a blend of hers and of those of the bride's he had just seen. *They both have that same sort of fresh, shiny, innocent look.* He fantasized about having his way with Kristen.

It's too bad she wouldn't go along with it. We could have been very good together. But she's so uptight. I guess that's what makes the chase so interesting. There's a chance she'll still resist giving in. I'll just have to see. . . . But if she won't have me, she won't have anyone.

*   *   *

Kristen sat in the backseat of her family's car, crammed between sacks of groceries and a pile of clothes that had been hurriedly gathered. Her mom and dad hadn't spoken to her much since they'd left home, heading for her grandparents' place thirty miles away.

She felt like a little girl who had done something so bad that her parents couldn't even talk to her about it until they'd had a chance to calm down.

She didn't want to talk, so she pretended to be asleep.

"I don't understand this at all," her dad complained to her mom. "This is a very busy time of year for me."

"I know it is, dear," her mom said.

Her dad continued. "We're running away from our home to go hide in the woods for who knows how long because some homicidal maniac gang leader might be coming here to kill us all. None of this makes sense. I mean, this is Idaho. Things like that don't happen here."

"I know. It's very confusing. As best as I can tell, it's all about the laptop. Chad gave it to her and then she gave it to Dutton. Apparently they found enough evidence on it to justify making an arrest. Chad's friends are dead now, and Chad is on the loose. He's got such a bad temper that Dutton thinks that if Chad suspects Kristen of cooperating with the police, he might come up here to get revenge."

"Do you think she slept with him?" her dad asked.

"Oh, I hope not. I'm not sure. She did talk to the bishop this afternoon though."

Her dad sighed. "That must mean she slept with Chad."

"What it means is that she's trying to put her life together."

Kristen couldn't take it any more. She sat up and leaned forward. "Mom? Dad? You know what? I didn't sleep with Chad."

She watched as her father's face and neck turned bright red. "I'm sorry," he said. "I thought you were asleep."

"It's okay. Can we talk when we get there?" Kristen asked.

"I think that would be a very good idea," her mom said.

Her grandparents' home was a large, two-story log house built fifty years earlier. It was located on a seldom-used gravel road that eventually led to Grand Teton National Park in Wyoming. In the winter the road was completely snowed in, and in the summer most tourists didn't even know it existed.

When they arrived, they lugged their belongings up the stairs to the porch and dumped them on the living room floor. Because Kristen's grandparents were on a mission and the house had been closed up, it had a cold, uninviting feel to it. At least that's how it felt to Kristen.

"Do you want to talk now?" she asked.

"If you're ready," her mom said.

Before they sat down, they pulled the plastic sheeting from the couch and chairs.

Her parents sat on the couch. Kristen sat down on the other side of the large room.

"You're so far away," her mom said.

Kristen pulled her chair across the room and placed it a few feet from the couch.

"Is that better?" she asked. Once again Kristen felt the way she had when she was in her early teens and had done something that displeased her mom and dad. *I'm not fourteen anymore,* she thought. *I can take charge of my life.*

"Dad, can we have a prayer first?" she asked.

"Sure." He glanced at his wife and daughter. "How about if I offer it?"

Her dad remained seated but leaned forward. He seemed in control as he asked Heavenly Father to help them as they talked, but when he prayed for protection, he had to stop. Kristen opened her eyes. Her dad had his lips shut tightly, and the muscles in his face were twitching as he struggled to keep his composure. Her mom reached out and touched his knee.

Kristen felt tears coming but was determined not to sniffle or make any sound that would give her away.

It was a long enough prayer that by the time her dad finished, the three of them were in control of their emotions.

"Go ahead," her dad said.

When she had been growing up, whenever she went to her bishop to talk to him about mistakes she'd made, she had never told her mom or dad any of the details, but this time she told them everything she had told

Bishop Brower. "So, the thing is," she concluded, "I drank alcohol. I came very close to getting a tattoo. I skipped church. I was in a dangerous situation with Chad. In a way I caused my friend Jonathan to get beaten up by Chad's friends. I know it's bad, but I've learned an important lesson."

"What have you learned?" her mom asked.

"You can't ever let your guard down. If all you want is to be accepted by your friends, no matter what they do, then you'll start drifting away from the teachings of the Church. That's what happened to me. Once I started to drift, I also quit reading the scriptures. I quit praying. I quit going to church. And I quit living the Word of Wisdom. It all happened so fast. I will never again stop doing the things that will help me have the influence of the Holy Ghost in my life."

Her dad nodded. "That is a great lesson to learn so early in your life."

She thought, *This may not be the beginning of my life—it might be near the end of my life.* But she didn't say anything because she didn't want to add to her parents' concern.

"Dad, can I have a father's blessing?"

He swallowed hard. "Yes, of course."

He stepped to the back of her chair, placed his hands on her head, and began.

He first expressed Heavenly Father's love for her. It wasn't long before she was crying, her mom was crying, and her dad was stopping every few words to try to keep his emotions in check.

At one point he paused.

Seconds went by.

Then, in a calm but firm voice, he said, "I bless you, Kristen, that guardian angels will be with you during this crisis in your life." He paused again. "They will protect your life until the time appointed by Heavenly Father."

When he closed the blessing, he turned quickly away, took out his handkerchief, and blew his nose and wiped his eyes. Then he took Kristen in his arms. For a long moment he said nothing, just held her tightly. Then he kissed her on the cheek and softly said, "I love you."

When they were done hugging, she and her mom hugged each other.

With their eyes red from tears, the three of them stood there as if they each wanted the moment to last.

Finally her mom said, "Well, let's get unpacked and see about getting us something to eat."

Kristen nodded and started to haul groceries into the kitchen.

She felt calm and at peace.

Later that night, when she was in the upstairs bedroom where she had always liked to stay when she was little, she reread the letter David Carpenter had sent her on his mission. It had arrived in California when she was seeing Chad. The first time she read the letter, it had been a reminder of how far she'd fallen from the teachings of the Church. At that time, she read it and quickly threw it in the garbage. Two days later, though, as she was emptying the trash, she saw the letter, and out of respect for David had decided to keep it.

Somehow David must have known I needed to know of his testimony. I'm grateful to him for listening to the Spirit, and I'm grateful to Heavenly Father for never giving up on me. That's what this letter means to me.

When she was done reading it, she carefully slipped it back into her scriptures.

*   *   *

As soon as his plane touched down in Idaho Falls, Dutton was on the phone to Delilah. "What have you got?"

"Plenty! We've been calling folks who contacted Motor Vehicles because they'd received new registration forms for cars they'd already sold. We found a woman in Brentwood. She sold her car to someone fitting Nieteri's description. We contacted state police for five western states asking for their help. If he's driving that car, and if he has the same plates on it, we'll nab him."

"Good work. Give me the description."

"Well, it's a four-door, gray 1998 Ford Taurus. I'll give you the license plate number."

He wrote it down.

"Tell everybody they're doing a great job. Now, if you haven't already, could you call local police stations along I-15 in Utah and Idaho and ask if anyone has reported their license plate stolen in the past day?" Dutton asked.

"That might take us a while."

"Yeah, I know."

Dutton ended the call, rented a car at the Idaho Falls airport, and half an hour later was heading north. He estimated it would take him just an hour to get to Ashton, and maybe another hour to find where Kristen and her family were staying.

After spending ten minutes on his cell phone listening to Kristen's mom and dad trying to give directions, he came to two conclusions: people in Idaho don't give directions very often, and when they do, they give them to people already familiar with the area. Somehow Dutton didn't think, "Go on that road until you pass a big red barn" was going to work well late at night.

*   *   *

Now in Ashton, Chad sat in his car and watched Kristen's home from across the highway and back in the woods. The place was dark.

A police car pulled into the driveway of the house. A potbellied cop got out, walked around the house, got back in his car and drove away.

Chad smiled. *Is that the best you can do, Pops? Where'd you get your training to be a cop?*

Why did the cop show up at all? Maybe Kristen's folks asked him to look after the place. But why? Kristen told me that people around here don't even lock up when they leave. So why have a cop stop by? Are they worried I might show up?

The fact the cop didn't stay might mean Kristen and her family are gone.

But where? There must be some way I can find out.

He drove to a convenience store in town. It was about to close.

He got himself a piece of frozen pizza and something to drink. While he waited for the microwave to heat up his pizza, he studied a tall guy with red hair and freckles working the cash register. Even though there were two customers waiting in line, the guy seemed to be in no hurry.

"So, how are things goin'?" the clerk asked.

"Goin' good. How about you?" the customer said.

"Oh, can't complain. Of course, it wouldn't do any good if I did."

In Chad's eyes, the guy laughed too much for such a stupid comment.

What a moron, he thought.

"Oh, your sister dropped by today. Won't be long now until she has that baby of hers, will it?"

"About a month."

"Time flies. I remember when we were in the school play together."

Chad finished his pizza. *The guy is an idiot, but maybe he knows something about Kristen and her family. I need to give him some reason to tell me where they are.*

In the frozen food section, he picked up a cake. And then he got in the checkout line.

"How's it goin'?" the clerk asked.

"Oh, can't complain," Chad mimicked. "I'm trying to find where you keep your birthday candles though. I need them for this cake."

"Yeah, sure, follow me."

Chad followed him down the aisle. "By any chance, do you happen to know Kristen Boone?"

"Are you kidding? We went to high school together."

"Wow, small world, right? She and I became good friends in California. Tomorrow is her birthday, so I thought I'd surprise her by coming out here for it, but when I went to her place, nobody was there. Do you know where they might have gone?"

The clerk handed Chad the candles. "Actually, I do. She and her mom came in today and bought a bunch of groceries. Kristen told me they were going away for a few days, but she told me not to tell anyone where."

"Look, give me a break. I've driven all the way from California just to see her. All I want to do is to wish her a happy birthday."

"She said she was going to her grandparents' place. Here, let me draw you a map of how to get there."

Five minutes later Chad left town with the cake, candles, and a map.

*　　*　　*

By the time Dutton arrived in Ashton, it was 12:30 at night and everything was closed. He looked over the vague directions Kristen's parents had given him, and then started on his way again.

A few minutes later, his cell phone rang. "Yeah," he said.

"Am I speaking to Officer Dutton?"

"That's right."

"The same Officer Dutton who commands the NORSAT investigative unit of the L.A. Sheriff's Department?"

"Who is this?"

"My name is Thomas Sheldrick. I'm a special investigator for the Federal Justice Department. I was given your name and was told you wrote a report about a group of officers in the Lynwood Station of the L.A. Sheriff's office who are taking the law into their own hands."

"Who told you that?"

"I'm really not at liberty to say."

"Where are you calling from, Mr. Sheldrick?"

"Actually, I'm in Hawaii with my wife and family. We're on vacation. You know what? Why do we haul our cell phones around with us all the time? It's like nobody can take a vacation anymore. We're all tethered to our jobs."

"It's a little after midnight for me, Mr. Sheldrick. In the first place, I have no way of knowing that you are who you say you are. Second, couldn't this wait until morning? And third, I'm kind of busy right now."

"You know, my wife told me not to call you while we were here. People get surly when someone calls them from Hawaii. It's like rubbing it in, so to speak."

"Are you sure you're an investigator, Mr. Sheldrick? Because you don't sound like the people I usually deal with."

"Oh, I'm an investigator all right, but at the same time, I have outside interests. Right now I am absolutely fascinated with pineapple."

Dutton came to a junction. He wasn't sure whether he should turn left or right. He slowed down and stopped the car.

Sheldrick continued, "I mean, what do we really know about pineapples?"

Looking at the map he had sketched from Kristen's parents' directions, Dutton found no indication of a junction. "Mr. Sheldrick, the truth is I'm lost."

"Oh, sorry! I do tend to ramble. I was talking about pineapples."

"I mean, I'm on a road and I'm lost."

"Where are you?"

"Idaho."

"What are you doing in Idaho? Don't you work for Los Angeles County? If you're in Idaho, I can't help you."

"That is very apparent to me. Look, I need to call someone for directions."

"When I get back to the States, and when you get back to California, I'd like to talk to you."

"If you agree not to talk about pineapples, I might agree."

"Not talk about pineapples! Wait until I tell my wife that! Because that's what she's been telling me since we set foot on Oahu."

"Good-bye, Mr. Sheldrick."

Dutton called Kristen on her cell phone.

"Hello?" she answered after three rings. She sounded as though she'd been asleep.

"I'm on my way, but I'm a little confused. I'm at a fork in the road and I don't know which way to go."

"Is there a sign?"

"No, there's no sign."

"I don't know where you are, but you must be on the wrong road. Look, why don't you just go back to Ashton, get a motel, and come out in the morning? Everything's fine here. Everyone's asleep except my cousin Ben. He's sitting in the living room with a shotgun on his lap. So we're in good shape. Besides, we really don't have a place for you to sleep tonight. We will tomorrow night because Ben is going home after you get here."

Dutton looked at his watch and sighed. The truth was that he did need some sleep. "Maybe I'll do that."

"Sleep tight, Dutton," she said before hanging up. "Don't let the bed bugs bite."

"Bed bugs? Is there something I should know about the motels in Ashton?" Dutton joked.

"No, that's just what my grandparents always used to tell me when I was a little girl and it was time for me to go to bed."

"Right. Well, good night, Kristen. I'll see you in the morning."

On the way back, he got lost again. He pulled into a public campground, set his wristwatch alarm for six-fifteen, leaned his head back, and soon fell asleep.

*   *   *

Chad was standing in the woods fifty yards from the house where Kristen and her folks were hiding out. Only one light was on, in the second floor of the large log-cabin home.

That's probably where Kristen is, he thought. *She's probably the night owl in her family. What would she think if she woke up with me sitting beside her on the bed? Would she be happy to see me? I bet she would. Who else has she ever had in her life like me? She'll never do better than me.*

I wonder if I can talk her into coming with me to Canada? We would be so good together. I would take good care of her. She would never want for money. I would make sure of that.

We'd get married eventually, if that was still important to her. Maybe we'd have children. I'd be such a good dad. I would teach my boys how to take care of themselves. Nobody would ever push my kids around on the playground.

He looked for a way he could get onto the roof. The fireplace chimney was made of natural rock and extended from the ground up. *I could climb that with no problem. Then all I have to do is go to her room, cut the screen with my knife, and slip in. Nobody would know I was there. It would give us a chance to talk about our future together. If she agrees to it, we could be in Canada by tomorrow night.*

Chad waited until the light went out and the house seemed quiet. He walked slowly and quietly to the chimney, then reached up and located a rock that would hold his weight. He put his foot on a lower rock and pulled himself up.

It was slow going. He had to test each rock as he climbed.

Ten minutes later he was crouched on the roof outside Kristen's room. It was quiet enough that he could hear her breathing.

Kristen, I'm coming to see you. I bet you'll be surprised.

He took his knife out of his pocket and was about to cut through the screen when he heard a noise coming from inside the house. He ducked down so that he wouldn't be seen.

Kristen's door opened. After what seemed an eternity, a man's voice said, "It looks like she's asleep." The door closed.

You idiot! Chad thought to himself. *You violated the first rule of law enforcement—never go into any situation without knowing what you're going to be facing. For all I know she has every cop in Idaho in that house. And why would I think that I could break into the house, show up in her room, and she wouldn't say anything? What is wrong with me? If I'm going to do this, I'm going to do it right.*

Surveillance first and then action. I've got to get out of here and look for my opportunity later.

He carefully climbed back down the chimney wall, one agonizing rock at a time until finally he stood on the ground again. He slipped back into the woods, hiked back to his car, and found a place where he could hide it from the road.

He looked at his watch. It was 2:30 in the morning.

Kristen, tomorrow is going to be such a big day for both of us. I know you might have gone to the cops with my laptop, but so what? Nobody's perfect. I can forgive everything you've done to mess up my life. All you have to do is agree to go with me to Canada.

You'll like Canada. There will be lots of trees and not very many people. Just like here. You'll fit right in, and we'll be together. Just the two of us. For better or worse, in sickness or in health.

But, hey, if you'd rather not come with me, that's okay too. It's your decision. You can be alive with me or you can be dead without me. I just want you to be happy.

CHAPTER TEN

Dutton woke up at four in the morning. It was still too dark to see any of the landmarks that would help him find where Kristen and her family were staying, but he couldn't get back to sleep.

It was still only a remote possibility that Chad would come to Idaho, but the business with the Lynwood Station was something that pressed heavily on his mind—whether or not he should cooperate with the federal investigation. He opened his suitcase and retrieved his Book of Mormon, turned on the dome light and began to read in Alma, chapter 61.

"Therefore, my beloved brother, Moroni, let us resist evil, and whatsoever evil we cannot resist with our words, yea, such as rebellions and dissensions, let us resist them with our swords, that we may retain our freedom, that we may rejoice in the great privilege of our church, and in the cause of our Redeemer and our God."

It seemed to be written just for him. Suddenly his mind was flooded with ideas. *That's it. We can and should resist evil with our words, and we must do that or we will lose our freedom. Don't citizens deserve to know that their law enforcement officers conduct themselves with the highest standards of integrity and honesty? Do we want out-of-control Gestapo cops in our society, dispensing their brand of justice, being both the judge and the jury?*

He read the passage several times and then stepped out of his car and knelt on the ground to say his morning prayers.

The night before, he had thought he was on a road that ran east and west. But when he stood up, he noticed the sun rising in what had seemed like north. He started laughing. Now he knew why he'd gotten lost.

Okay, now all I have to do is find Kristen, he thought.

* * *

Chad had spent the night in his car in a secluded area on a hill where he had a good view of the house but could remain undetected.

When he woke up, it was light enough to see the house. *I can wait for the right time. So much of police work is surveillance and waiting, but that's okay. If you wait long enough, there's always an opportunity.*

* * *

Kristen woke up early, got dressed, and went downstairs. Everyone was asleep.

She felt relieved to know that Dutton had arrived and was in a motel room in Ashton. *I hope he doesn't have any trouble finding us like he did last night,* she thought.

After opening the refrigerator, she remembered they'd run out of milk the night before.

I'll go into town, pick up some milk, get Dutton up, and have him follow me back, she thought.

She went into the living room. Her cousin Ben was asleep on the couch.

"Ben, you want to go with me to town? We're out of milk."

Ben mumbled something and turned away from her.

"It's okay. I'll go by myself."

She grabbed her keys and walked quietly out the door to her car. *I'll be back before anyone knows I'm gone. And when I come back, I'll have Dutton with me. We'll all be relieved to have him here.*

*　　*　　*

To Chad there was only one explanation for why Kristen would be sneaking out of the house. *It was her folks' idea to keep her away from me,* he thought, *but now she's out looking for me. Well, Kristen, don't worry. This is your lucky day! Your bad boy is here!*

He backed his car out of the wooded area and headed after her. He drove slowly past the house where she'd been staying. He didn't want to wake anyone up.

It won't do for her to think I'm chasing her. She might panic and think I'm mad at her and want to hurt her. I need to have her stop and not try to get away from me. How can I do that?

Suddenly the answer was obvious. He would do what had always worked before. He would be a police officer.

He stopped and outfitted himself as a police officer, slapped a police flashing light unit on the roof of the car, and took off after her.

A short time later, he pulled up behind her car and turned the police light on. She slowed down and stopped.

He got out, walked up to her car, smiled, and said, "Good morning, Kristen. Been playing much solitaire lately?"

Her eyes got big and she reached for the lock button, but he yanked the door open before she could get to it. "Relax, I'm not going to hurt you. I'm on my way to Canada, and I thought I'd drop by and see you. I just want to talk. Move over so I can get in."

She slid over to the passenger seat, and he got into the car. "Just one question and then I'll be going. You told me the only thing you'd used my laptop for was to play solitaire. Is that true, or were you lying?"

She closed her eyes and sighed. "I never did play solitaire on it."

"You see there? That explains everything. Because if you had, it would've showed up as a favorite program. So that clears up everything. Thank you. Well, I'd better be going." He opened the door as if he were about to leave. "Oh, just one thing before I go. I want you to know I've changed a lot. I look at things differently now. You know, about life for example. I don't know if you've heard or not, but Mike, Tyler, and Andy were killed. Think of it, my three best friends—one minute they were there, and then all of a sudden, they were gone. You knew about it, didn't you?"

"No. I'm very sorry to hear it."

He smiled. "I can always tell when you're lying. Of course you knew. In a way, you caused it to happen. You turned my laptop over to the cops, didn't you?"

"No."

"Yes, you did. You see how well I'm taking it? I mean, the old Chad would've hit you for lying, but I'm not like that anymore. I'm a changed man, Kristen. And now all I want to do is to start all over."

She had her arms wrapped tightly around herself and was hunched over with her gaze on the floorboard. "That's good."

"You know what? My whole trip up here was made possible by people like you. I bought a car from a woman in Utah. I went out to her house. She has the cutest little girl in the world. I couldn't help but think that little girl would look like our daughter. Does that surprise you that I would be thinking about that?"

Her breathing was now a series of short gasps.

"Relax, okay? Then, just outside of Idaho Falls, I ended up going to a wedding reception. I even went through the line and everything. The bride was so hot. Oh, excuse me, I mean that in a good way. I mean, think about it. I bet she saved herself just for him. Isn't that a great gift for a girl to offer a guy?"

"Please don't hurt me, Chad," she pleaded.

"No, look, don't worry. This is the new Chad talking. I've changed. I want to settle down and get married and have a family. I want us to get married."

She shook her head. "I can't marry you."

"But I've changed. You just need to spend some time with me, and you'll see it. Come with me to Canada. I promise I won't lay a hand on you. We'll spend a few weeks together and if, at the end of that time, you still feel the same way, well then, you can go home. I just want you to see how much I've changed. Have you ever been to Canada?"

She shook her head.

"Well, then, you're going to love it. There is just one problem, though, but we can work that out. I have a fake I.D. so there will be no problem for me to get in, but we'll have to have you sneak across the border and then I'll pick you up. But other than that, I don't see any problem. And I've got plenty of money to get by until we can get jobs. So what do you say?"

He grabbed her arm and pulled her to him, kissing her hard on the mouth. When she tried to pull away, he let go of her. "Relax, okay? I'm not going to hurt you. I could, but I won't, because I'm a changed man."

Her eyes were closed and she was struggling to keep from crying.

"You're wasting my time," Chad said. "I need a decision."

"I can't go with you, and I can't marry you."

He laughed. "*Can't* is such a negative word. Let me put it this way. Either you come with me and be my wife or else I will kill you."

"I won't go with you."

"Even if it means you'll die if you don't?"

"Yes."

"That is so admirable of you, Kristen. What a great church you belong to, to build that kind of loyalty to principles. I really do want to join someday. I'm almost there, if I just had a woman who could help me make the changes I need to make in my life."

"It won't be me."

"I can't believe you mean that. Here, let me illustrate the point I'm trying to make." He grabbed her arm again, opened the door with his left hand, and dragged her out of the car. "We need to take a walk. It's time for an object lesson."

He stepped beside her, put his arm around her waist, and shoved his gun into her cheek. "Let's take a walk, Sweetheart. I'm not going to hurt you. I just want to teach you an important lesson. You want to know what that lesson is? When it comes to crunch time, people will always choose life over death. You don't understand that yet, do you? You probably think this is some kind of Bible study lesson, where everybody goes home afterwards and eats roast beef. Well, that's not what this is. Not this time."

He put the gun in the pocket of his jacket, grabbed her hand, and led her into the woods.

"Chad, don't hurt me."

"I'm not going to force myself on you, Kristen, if that's what you're worried about. I'm not that kind of guy. Girls come on to *me*. That's the way it's always been. So don't worry about that. Of course I may have to shoot you, but I promise that I will not violate you. Even the old Chad has standards. I just wish you'd agree to come with me so you can see how much I've changed. I think you'd be very pleased."

"Please, Chad, let me go. I promise I won't say anything to anyone."

"That's for sure. I can guarantee that."

They came to a cliff with a drop of about fifty feet.

"Let's sit here and talk." He made her sit beside him on the rocks, their legs dangling over the edge of the cliff.

"I'm going to let go of you now," he said. "But if you try to run away, I'll shoot you and throw your body off the cliff. I assume you don't want me to do that, so just stay here by my side."

When he released his grip, she didn't try to escape. "That's my good girl," he said, raising her face to him.

She wouldn't look at him.

"It's a beautiful morning, isn't it?" he said, gesturing toward the lush, dewy pastures and a line of trees along a creek in the distance. "I don't understand how some people say there's no God, do you? You can just look around on a day like this and know that he's there, looking down on us. I wonder if he can see us? I bet he's happy that we're together, don't you?"

He waited for a reply. "You can break in here anytime you want. It's what we call a conversation." His voice was flat and hard.

She shook her head.

He smiled. "Well, no matter. Have I ever told you about my dad?"

"No, you never have."

"He's a cop, just like me." He chuckled. "Well, not exactly like me, of course. When I was growing up, he was my hero. He always worked nights. I remember going into my parents' bedroom just to watch my dad get ready for work. It was every boy's dream. You know, the gun, the handcuffs, the badge, what more could anyone want? But more than anything I wanted to be just like him. Mike, Tyler, and Andy were the same, too. All of us were sons of cops, wanting to grow up and become like our dads."

She glanced at him. "What happened?"

"Well, when I was twelve, my mom found out that dear old dad was seeing someone on the side. He'd been doing it most of their married life. Some of the nights we thought he was working so hard, he was spending his time with her. Can you believe that? One night he told my mom he didn't want to be married anymore, and then he got in his car and drove away."

"I'm sorry, Chad."

"My mom tried to tell me that he wasn't divorcing me, that he would still be my dad, and that he'd come and watch me play basketball or football, but he never came. I used to look up in the stands hoping to see him. But he was never there."

He sighed. "You might guess that made me just a little bitter about a career in law enforcement. But I still loved the guns and the badges and the handcuffs. Years later Mike, Tyler, Andy, and I came up with a great idea. We'd help the cops by doing drug raids. Instead of the money going to the police departments, we thought it would only be right if it went to us. After all, we were the ones in the firing line, so to speak."

Kristen began to cry.

He looked at her. "I'm amazed my little story has touched you so deeply."

"It's not that."

"What is it then?"

"You're not going to let me go, are you? That's why you feel like you can tell me everything. I either have to go with you, or you'll kill me."

"Good logic, girl. You'd make a good cop. Now let me tell you about my mom and her revolving husband problem. What's it been? Five, six, seven?—I've lost count. But it's a story I don't get much chance to tell."

*   *   *

Dutton pulled up behind the two cars parked on the side of the gravel road. One of them matched the description of the car Delilah had told him Chad might be driving, even though it had Utah plates. There was a flashing police light unit on the top of the car.

He checked the registration of the first car. It was registered to Kristen's dad.

Going around to the other side of the cars, he saw tracks in the wet grass, leading off the road and into the woods. Drawing his weapon, he slowly made his way into the forest.

He moved slowly. He didn't want to spook Chad.

*   *   *

"So that's the story of my life," Chad said. "I hope you can see how it caused me to make some bad choices, for which I am now profoundly sorry."

"Chad, if you're sorry, give yourself up."

"Well, I would, Sweetheart, but they are very likely to want me to serve jail time. And I really don't think I could stand that."

"I'll write to you."

"Really? That would be great."

"I do see good in you, Chad."

"I'm so glad to hear you say that. You're an amazing girl, Kristen. That was so obvious the first time I saw you. In a way I guess you could say you've inspired me to be better."

"Then let's go back so you can turn yourself in."

"But, the thing is, I don't have to do that. We can go to Canada and just start over again, you and me." He pulled his wallet out of his pocket and showed her his fake I.D. "Right now, I'm Justin Alexander. You could be Mrs. Alexander. How does that sound?"

"But we'd spend the rest of our lives worrying that they'd find you."

"Did you say *we*? I take that as a very favorable sign."

"I meant that hypothetically."

"Yes, I know. You do that a lot. But, the truth is, you can't live a hypothetical life. Life comes the way it comes. And you have to learn to go with the flow. That's what I want you to learn today."

He got on his knees. "Kristen, I've poured out my soul to you, more so to you than anyone else. I know I'm not perfect, but you can see I want to change. So, will you come with me to Canada? I promise you we'll live like brother and sister until you're ready for something . . . well, more interesting."

"I can't do that, Chad."

"Why not?"

"Because . . . you scare me."

"Me?" he asked with an innocent smile. "You're scared of me? There's nothing to be scared of. I'm a changed man."

"Did you videotape the girls in your apartment?"

"No, of course not. Who told you that?"

"Dutton."

"Dutton? The same Dutton who works for NORSAT? I know this man, Kristen. You can't believe anything he'd tell you."

"Did you videotape us when I was in your apartment?"

"Absolutely not. And even if I had, it would've been a complete waste of technology. Because nothing happened. But that's good, okay? Because you always set a good example. And I admire that, because I'm a changed man. Let's go."

He stood up and then helped her get up. "Before we head off to the police so I can turn myself in and spend the next twenty years reading the letters you send me in prison, let me allow the old Chad to say a few words. Is that all right?"

Holding his gun in his right hand, he quickly stepped behind her, put his right arm around her neck, bent her left arm behind her and wrenched it toward her shoulder blade.

"You're hurting me," she whimpered.

"I don't care!" he said, his voice loud and harsh. "This is the old Chad now! Do you have any idea how you've wrecked my life? Because you went to the cops, you got Mike, Tyler, and Andy killed. I am now a hunted man and will be for the rest of my life. You destroyed a setup that brought thousands of dollars to me every week. I can never go back to L.A. again. The girls I used to know are now off limits to me. I have to spend the rest of my life in some log cabin in the middle of nowhere. You've been nothing but trouble to me. Do you know what that means?" He increased the pressure around her neck and wrenched her arm even harder.

"No," she gasped.

He shouted in her ear. "It means you have no right to live! That's what it means!" He twisted her arm again, and she cried out. "I don't like hurting you, Kristen, but sometimes people need to learn a lesson."

He let go of her arm and used his left hand to grab the waistband in the back of her jeans.

"Okay, Sweetheart, say a little prayer. Because you're going over the cliff. Are you praying real hard? On the count of three . . . ready? One . . . two . . . three! Good-bye, Kristen! Say hello to God for me, okay?"

"No, Chad, please!"

He gave her enough of a jolt forward to make her think he was pushing her off the cliff. Just before she would have tumbled over the edge, he used the hold on her waistband to jerk her back from falling.

She screamed. "No, please don't!" she pleaded.

He laughed. "Hey, you know me better than that! I was just kidding. You know I would never hurt you. I'm just trying to teach you a very important lesson. One more time, Kristen, are you coming with me to Canada or not? Make up your mind."

Her breathing was now coming in short, labored gasps.

"What's your answer?" he shouted.

"No."

He shook her as he yelled at her. "No? Are you out of your mind? Even a stupid fox in a trap will chew off his paw just to live another day. What is wrong with you? Okay, let's do it again, and this time, I'm really going to throw you off the cliff. On the count of three . . . one . . . two . . . three!"

Again he pushed her forward then yanked her back. By now, she was crying hysterically.

He laughed. "Makes you wonder if I'll ever get tired of this, doesn't it? One . . . two . . . three . . . 'Bye, Kristen!"

Kristen screamed.

*   *   *

The first time Dutton heard Kristen scream, he broke into a run. As he hurried to find her, he heard her scream a second time.

As he approached a clearing, he saw Chad and Kristen at the edge of the cliff. She was sobbing and begging for him to stop.

"You love this, don't you? I know, let's do it again!" Chad yelled and then pushed her forward then yanked her back. Once again she screamed.

Dutton couldn't shoot because the bullet would go through Chad into Kristen, and even if it didn't, shooting Chad could still result in Kristen going over the cliff.

He decided to distract Chad. "It's all over, Chad!" he shouted.

Chad quickly turned around, holding Kristen in front of him as he faced the officer. "Hey, it's Dutton, everybody! The officer who never fires his gun. I'm glad it's you, Dutton. All of us criminals feel so much safer knowing you're around."

"You're surrounded. Put down your gun and step away from the girl."

Chad laughed. "Surrounded? By what? Chipmunks?"

"Drop your gun and step away from her, and everything will be all right."

"Why would I want to do that, when the only reason I came here was to get her?"

"Kristen's done nothing to you. There's no reason to harm her."

"I know what she did with the laptop."

"You're young. Get yourself a good lawyer, and you might walk. And even if you're convicted, you'll only serve a few years and then you'll be paroled."

"Yeah, sure. I've heard all that from Kristen." He sighed. "But you know what? You're both probably right. Lord knows I don't want to die, especially in Idaho. Okay, Dutton, you win." He lowered his gun and stepped away from Kristen. "I'm going to set my gun down, nice and easy."

He stooped and set the gun on the ground. "There now, that's better. I guess we're all breathing a lot easier right now, aren't we?" He turned to face Kristen. "You okay, Sweetheart? Sorry to scare you. I would never hurt you, you know that."

Still facing the edge of the cliff, with her back still to Chad, Kristen turned slightly to look at Chad and Dutton behind her. Suddenly Chad whirled, using his forearm to hit Kristen in the back of her knees, causing her legs to buckle, and pitching her toward the cliff.

With Dutton's attention diverted to Kristen as she desperately tried to grab something that would keep her from falling off the cliff, Chad reached down, picked up his gun, and fired at Dutton.

The bullet missed. Dutton then fired twice. The impact of the bullets knocked Chad backward. He lost his footing, flailed at the air, and fell off the cliff.

Dutton ran to Kristen, who was lying on her stomach, hanging onto the rounded edge of a boulder, her legs dangling over the cliff. Dutton got hold of her arms and pulled her to safety. As soon as he got her to her feet, she crumpled into a ball, trembling and crying.

Dutton found another route to the bottom of the cliff to verify that Chad was dead. A few minutes later he returned to Kristen, who was still sobbing. He sat beside her and patted her on the back. "He's not going to hurt you anymore."

"Is he dead?"

"Yes. I had no choice."

"I know. I'm glad he's dead."

Half an hour later he helped her back to her car, then called the sheriff's office and reported the shooting.

Next he called Kristen's folks and talked to her dad. "This is Dutton. First of all, everything is fine. Kristen hasn't been hurt, but Chad Nieteri kidnapped her for a short time. When I found them, Chad was endangering her life, and there was a shoot-out. Chad is dead. I've called the sheriff, and he's on the way. Kristen is fine, but she needs to answer some questions before they'll let her go. We shouldn't be much longer. I'll make sure she gets back to you safely."

Half an hour later the sheriff, a deputy, a tow truck, and an ambulance showed up.

An hour later the sheriff let Dutton and Kristen go.

Dutton got into his car and followed Kristen as she drove her car to her grandparents' house. When they pulled into the yard, everyone ran out and threw their arms around Kristen.

They went into the house and left Dutton standing in the driveway. He felt like an intruder and wondered if it would be better for Kristen if he left. He got back into his car.

Kristen saw him from the window and sent her dad out to talk to him.

Dutton rolled down his window.

"You're welcome to stay," her dad said.

"Well, that's very kind of you, but I really do need to get back to my family."

Kristen's dad warmly shook Dutton's hand. "Thank you for saving my daughter's life."

"I'm just glad I got there in time."

"If I can ever help you, call me. If you ever need anything, just call. If you and your wife ever want to take a vacation in Idaho, let us know. You can stay here. My folks don't get back from their mission for six months, so it's available to you, free of charge. Any time. Please let us know. You'll always be important to us."

"Thank you. I'll remember your offer," Dutton said and then left.

Taking a life is never easy, and going over it in his mind later, Dutton couldn't remember how he got back to Ashton. At eight that night, when he reached Rexburg, he had calmed down enough to realize he was both hungry and exhausted.

He pulled into a restaurant, had a good meal, and then walked next door and booked a room for the night.

He shaved, took a shower, then called Laura to tell her he was all right, sparing some of the details until he got home so she wouldn't worry.

Once again he read in Alma about the necessity of fighting evil with our words. He knew he had to make a decision about the Viking report.

At 10:30 that night he called Sheldrick's cell phone.

"This is Dutton. I'm ready to talk to you now," he said.

"Wonderful! I'm so pleased. My family and I are at the Honolulu airport. We're taking the red-eye to San Francisco tonight. Where and when do you want to meet?"

"Not in L.A."

"Hold on . . . Okay, we're flying from San Francisco to Salt Lake City in the morning. We'll arrive in Utah at one o'clock, and I see we have a two-hour layover. How would that work for you?"

"Good."

"Where do you want to meet?"

"I'll meet your flight."

"Perfect! We'll bring you some pineapples."

"How will I recognize you?"

"You won't have any trouble. We're a large family and not easily missed. I look forward to meeting you. And let me say, most warmly, welcome aboard!"

A few minutes later, after he ended the call, Dutton shook his head. *I have no way of knowing how this will turn out. I wonder if Captain Moroni ever felt this way.*

CHAPTER ELEVEN

The next day at the Salt Lake City Airport, Dutton waited for Thomas Sheldrick and his family to exit the concourse and come into the baggage claim area. Since Sheldrick said he had a big family, Dutton was watching for a family with several children.

A man weighing close to three hundred pounds and standing at least six-foot-three, with a woman at his side who seemed even bigger, entered the terminal. A boy, around ten years old, who must have weighed at least a hundred and fifty pounds, followed close behind them. Now Dutton knew what Sheldrick meant by a "large family."

The three of them all wore Bermuda shorts, flip-flops, and bright Hawaiian shirts. Each of them wore a lei. The woman also held a lei in her hand, and the man carried with him a pineapple gift pack.

The man scanned the crowd and then fixed his gaze on Dutton. "There he is."

He made his way through the crowd and threw his arms around Dutton. "Aloha, my friend."

"Sheldrick?" Dutton asked.

"I am! And this is my wife, Nancy, and our son, Phillip."

"Aloha!" his wife said, placing a lei around Dutton's neck and kissing him on the cheek.

"Look what we have for you!" Sheldrick said, handing Dutton the gift pack of pineapple. "We brought it all the way from Hawaii!"

"Thank you." Dutton looked at his watch. "My flight leaves in an hour."

"Spoken like a mainlander. Work, work, work, right? Keep your nose to the grindstone! You really need a trip to Hawaii! It would do wonders for you. Well, no matter. I've arranged for a place where we can meet. Let's go."

Leaving Mrs. Sheldrick and Phillip in the waiting area, the two men rode a courtesy vehicle driven by a tight-lipped driver, ending up in an obscure office in the main terminal. A waiting security guard unlocked the door and let them in.

"Wait for us," Sheldrick said to the driver.

The room was empty except for a table and two chairs. A large knife lay on the table.

"Please sit down."

As Dutton sat down, Sheldrick used the knife to cut the bark off one of the pineapples, then sliced it into pieces. He inhaled deeply. "Smell that. It's like holding a little bit of Hawaii in your hands." He handed Dutton a slice of pineapple. "I should've asked for napkins, I can see that now. Oh, well, no matter. Now, tell me what you know."

Dutton ate the slice of pineapple and reached for his handkerchief. Wiping the juice off his hands and mouth, he said, "Three months ago I was asked to speak to a man who used to work at the Lynwood Station."

"Oh, yes. The infamous Lynwood Station," Sheldrick said.

"Right. This former officer had been convicted of shooting a pregnant woman during an unauthorized raid on a crack house and is now being held in the county jail. He told me that a secret group of officers at the Lynwood Station calling themselves the Vikings had been planting evidence, falsifying reports, and, in effect, taking the law into their own hands."

"What did you do with that information?" Sheldrick asked.

"I called my supervisor and asked him to listen to this guy. He came and listened and said he'd take care of it."

"What did he do?"

"Nothing. After waiting a few days, I wrote a report and sent it to headquarters."

"Why did you write a report?"

"So someone like you wouldn't come after me, asking why I hadn't done anything with the information."

Sheldrick nodded. "So you were covering your backside, right?"

"Right."

"When I do that, it takes a lot of covering!" At first Sheldrick laughed, but then, noticing that Dutton wasn't even smiling, he cleared his throat and then became serious. "I'll need the name of this officer."

"Robert Armstrong. But if the Vikings find out that he's implicated them, they'll kill him."

"I'll put him into the witness protection program. I can have him out in three hours."

"How can you get it done that fast?"

"I have authority to make things happen, my friend. Have another piece of pineapple."

"No thanks, I've had enough."

Sheldrick raised his voice. "I would very much like you to have another piece of pineapple. Especially since I had to lug it all the way from Hawaii."

Dutton sighed and dutifully took another piece.

Sheldrick playfully jabbed his finger into Dutton's chest. "You see what just happened? You didn't want any more pineapple, but I insisted, so you went along with it. That's what I do. It's no good just to have power and authority. You must also have a commanding presence and the will to get what you want. That's why I am where I am. It's not because I can run fast, that's for sure." He looked at his watch. "In three hours your officer will be on his way to a new life. Where is this Robert Armstrong being incarcerated?"

"The L.A. County Jail."

"That's all I need."

"How long will your investigation of the Lynwood Station take?" Dutton asked.

"Maybe a month, maybe longer. It's hard to say."

"I would think it would take much longer than that," Dutton said.

"I'm a specialty man with unlimited resources. I don't work on just any case. Only the ones that infringe on the rights of everyday citizens. My job gives me great satisfaction."

"I'm a little concerned about what will happen to me once it becomes known that I've cooperated with your investigation."

"I don't reveal my sources to anyone."

"I think they'll be able to figure it out."

"Do you want me to say that there's no danger in what you're doing? I can't say that. I'll do my best to finish my work as quickly as possible. We'll clean out the corruption as deep as it goes."

"And until then?"

"I would think that would be obvious. Watch your back."

*   *   *

During his flight to L.A., Dutton's mind raced through the jumbled fragments of what used to be a well-ordered life. When the plane landed, all he wanted to do was go home, hug his family, eat a home-cooked meal, put the kids to bed, and then stay up late having cookies and milk with Laura in the kitchen. She was the one he always went to when he needed someone to help him sort things out.

His flight landed on time. He was one of the first to stand up and grab his carry-on bag after the plane docked. Once in the terminal, he walked fast and soon outdistanced the other passengers from his flight.

As he was about to leave the security area, he saw a group of reporters and a TV crew from an L.A. TV station. He glanced behind him, wondering if there had been a celebrity on his flight.

"There he is!" the cameraman from the TV station said to a young, self-absorbed beauty with a microphone in her hand.

Dutton realized that the news team was waiting for him.

"Officer Dutton, I'm Colleen Ferrell from Channel 8 News. I'd like to interview you regarding your heroic action in Idaho. I want you to tell our viewers what it was like being in a gunfight with the notorious Chad Nieteri."

Dutton's mouth dropped. "How do you know about that?"

"Later. We'll be on the air in five seconds, sir. Five, four, three, two." She turned up her smile and enthusiasm and faced the TV camera. "This is Colleen Ferrell, standing here with Commander Kendall Dutton of the Los Angeles County Sheriff's office, who yesterday was involved in the fatal gunfight with fugitive Chad Nieteri. Nieteri was, of course, the leader of a local gang calling itself the Monkey Boys, who after escaping arrest, led law enforcement officers on a thousand-mile chase from Los Angeles to Idaho. It was there that Officer Dutton finally cornered Nieteri and Kristen Boone, a young woman who had been his classmate at UCLA. Officer Dutton tracked them to their hideout in northeastern Idaho. Commander Dutton, I understand you shot Nieteri twice in the chest. What was it like for you to be trading bullets with this notorious gang leader?"

"With all due respect, ma'am, you don't have your story straight."

"You did shoot and kill Nieteri, didn't you?"

"Yes."

"What was that like?"

"I had no choice. He was about to throw Kristen Boone off a cliff."

"Really? Was it a lovers' spat that got out of control?"

"No, no, that's not the way it was."

"These two will remind many of our viewers of outlaw lovers Bonnie and Clyde, who terrorized store owners, robbed banks, and were themselves gunned down by police officers in 1934."

"Let me make this clear to you," Dutton said, "Miss Boone was not a member of the Monkey Boys gang. She did not know of their illegal activities. Every indication we have is that she and Nieteri met only a short time ago and were just friends. Any other spin you might put on this is dead wrong. To imply otherwise would be totally irresponsible. Good night."

As he walked away, he could hear Colleen Ferrell wrapping up the interview. "Are Kristen Boone and Chad Nieteri a modern-day version of Bonnie and Clyde? We will answer that question for our viewers. Even as we speak, our news team is on its way to tiny Ashton, Idaho, where they will attempt to interview Kristen Boone in order to learn the truth about her relationship with the outlaw Chad Nieteri, who as you know was yesterday finally gunned down by police while resisting arrest. This is Colleen Ferrell, reporting live from LAX."

Dutton hurried to where he had parked his car. As he put his key in the lock, a man stepped out of the shadows. Dutton reached for his gun.

"Take it easy, Dutton. So, how's our TV celebrity?"

Dutton recognized the voice immediately. It was Morgan, the man who had botched the attempt to arrest the Monkey Boys.

Morgan stepped into the light.

"Did you set me up for that interview?" Dutton asked.

Morgan smiled. "You seemed bitter I was getting all the glory. I wanted you to share the spotlight with me. It's funny how it has all worked out, isn't it? You kill a few, I kill a few."

"You arranged the publicity about my shooting Nieteri so I wouldn't complain about you, didn't you?"

"That might have been a small part of it. You see, Dutton, the public can't tell the difference between what you consider a justified killing and what I consider justified. To me if I stop a car and tell everyone to throw out their guns, and, instead of doing that, they try to make a run for it, then I'm justified in whatever I do after that."

"Four people could be alive today if it weren't for you."

"Right. And they'd get lawyers, and the lawyers would muddy the water, and then some sympathetic jury would feel sorry for those poor misunderstood boys, and they'd either get a few months in a country-club prison or else they'd end up walking away free men. That's not right, Dutton. That's not why we put our lives on the line."

"I always feel like I need a shower after talking with you, Morgan. Maybe it would be better if we kept our distance."

"The truth is, Dutton, I'm almost the only friend you've got right now."

Dutton shook his head. "How do you figure that?"

"There are a lot of people nervous about your report on the Vikings. A lot of people worried about what you're going to do with it. If you're not careful, you could put the sheriff's office in a very bad light."

"How do you know about that?"

"Everyone knows. They're all just too polite to tell you. Some are on your side, but others, in high positions, are worried about what you'll do. If word gets out to the media that you had warned the powers that be well before Mr. Sanchez was brutally attacked, the public will demand action. You can see how that would upset some people in the sheriff's department."

"What's your point, Morgan?"

"If you want to protect your career, agree to whatever they ask of you. Play the game, Dutton, like everyone else does."

"Why isn't it a surprise to hear you say that? You make me ashamed to be in law enforcement. I'm tired, Morgan, I've had a hard few days. I need to go home to my family."

"Look, your family is in this, too. If I know about your report, you can be sure the Vikings know about it also. Who's going to protect your family twenty-four/seven? You? Impossible. Local law enforcement? Dream on. In fact, for all you know, they might be the ones doing the hunting. As unlikely as it may appear to you, I am on your side."

"If I need your help, I'll call you. Otherwise, stay away from me," Dutton said emphatically, climbing into his car and driving away.

On the way home, he kept looking in his rearview mirror, trying to determine if anyone was following him. His head was pounding and the muscles in his neck and shoulders were cable tight.

He grabbed his cell phone and called Kristen's cell phone number.

"Hello?" she said.

"This is Dutton. There's a TV news team from L.A. on their way to interview you."

"Do I have to talk to them?"

"No."

"Then I won't."

"The trouble is, if you don't, they'll make up their own story, and it might not be favorable to you."

"So what should I do?" she asked.

"Talk to them. Tell them the truth. That you and Chad were just friends."

"Should I tell them about the laptop?"

"You might as well." He paused. "The woman who interviewed me implied you knew everything that Chad was doing, and that you two were lovers. Neither one is true, is it?"

"Am I going to be answering that question for the rest of my life?" she cried out.

"No, just for a little while. The more honest and open you are now the less interest the media will have in you later on."

"I didn't do anything wrong."

"I know."

There was a long break and then Kristen said, "A car just pulled into the driveway. They don't look like they're from around here. One guy is taking a TV camera out of the trunk."

"That's them. Good luck."

"This will never be over, will it?" she asked before ending the call.

When Dutton pulled into his driveway, there was a TV news team from another local station waiting outside his house. They ran over to him as he got out of his car.

"I can't talk to you now," he said.

"When can you talk to us?"

"Tomorrow. I'll have a news conference and everyone can ask whatever questions they want. Leave your name and I'll have my secretary call you to arrange the time and place."

"That's fine, but we need something now. We're on the air in twelve minutes."

"I can't help you. I haven't seen my wife and family for days."

"Just one question if I may." Dutton turned to the camera. "Officer Dutton, do you think it is a commentary on what kind of men are working for the Los Angeles Police Department that four of their sons would be able to get away with what they did for so long?"

"It's not a commentary on anything. There are thousands of law enforcement personnel in this area. We know of four families where there was apparently a problem. I just don't think you can make a generalization based on four individuals."

"We understand you have been critical of the way the initial arrest attempt was made, in which three of the gang were killed in a shoot-out with L.A. police officers. Would you care to comment on your concerns?"

"No, I would not. Look, I need to worry about my own family now, so if you'll excuse me."

"Sir, one more question."

Dutton didn't wait around long enough to find out what the question was.

Laura was at the door as he came in. "Do you want me to kiss you in front of the camera?" Laura asked. "They've been here for two hours, and the phone has been ringing off the hook."

"I'm sorry," he said as he shut the door.

"I'm sorry too. When we talked yesterday, you didn't tell me Chad Nieteri had shot at you."

"I didn't want you to worry."

"How many other people have shot at you that I don't know about?" she asked.

"Nobody else."

"I need to know everything. Because I don't want to hear about it from the news stations."

"All right, from now on I'll tell you."

She came to him. He held her in his arms and kissed her. "I hope they got that," she said, glancing toward the front window.

"News flash. Dutton is crazy about his wife and kids. By the way, where are the kids?"

"Adam and Abigail are spending the night with friends. My mom has Gabe. I didn't want them being hunted down by TV news reporters."

He smiled. "So we're all alone?" he asked.

"Just us and a couple of million late-night TV viewers."

"We could close the drapes."

"But I'll still know they're there."

"How about if I shoot them? No jury would convict."

She laughed. "That might work, but the neighbors might talk when they wake up in the morning and see the dead bodies on our front lawn."

"I suppose."

She looked up at him. "What the heck? I'm willing to risk it."

He reached for his gun. "I'll be back in a minute."

She started giggling. "Not that!"

"What then?"

"The other."

"The other?"

"Yes, the other."

"Really? Well, things are looking up after all. Let's synchronize our watches. I'll meet you in ten minutes."

Dutton smiled as he pulled the drapes and they got ready for bed.

*   *   *

The next morning Dutton was smiling as he came into the office.

"Oh, can I have your autograph?" Delilah teased.

"You must have watched the news last night," he said.

She nodded with a grin. "You do the 'deer in the headlights' look so well, Chief."

"I'm glad to be back, Delilah. I've missed your hammering me."

"Well, looks like I'll have to stand in line today. As soon as I came in this morning, I got a call from DeSoto. He wants to see you in his office immediately. I'm no psychic, but to me it sounded like he wanted to rip your head off."

"Can you set up a news conference for me at two o'clock?"

"Okay."

DeSoto didn't even smile when Dutton showed up at his office. "Sit down," he grumbled.

Dutton sat down.

"Yesterday Robert Armstrong was released from jail and remanded over to federal jurisdiction. What do you know about that?"

"I don't work for the feds," Dutton said. "Why don't you ask them?"

"Because I'm asking you! Why would they want Armstrong?"

"How should I know?"

"Don't play games with me! Armstrong is the only one willing to testify about the Vikings, and you wrote about him in your report. What have you done? Have you talked to the feds?"

Dutton didn't know how to respond to the question. He didn't usually resort to lying, but was considering it as an option now. "I didn't go to the feds."

"How did they know about Armstrong then?"

"Why don't you ask them?" Dutton said angrily.

"Who do you suggest I ask? A guy named Sheldrick authorized it, but he's not local, and nobody knows how to get hold of him. We're getting stonewalled by the feds. Nobody knows anything."

"Too bad."

"I checked the itinerary for your flights. Why did you spend an extra day in Salt Lake City? Did you meet with Sheldrick?"

Dutton decided it was too much trouble to lie. "Yes, I did."

DeSoto banged the table with his fist and swore. "I knew it! What were you thinking? Do you have any idea how much damage you could do to the department?"

"Do you have any idea how much damage the Vikings have done to innocent citizens? Why isn't that your concern, DeSoto? Why aren't you leading the charge to rid the department of rogue cops?"

"That's it! You're fired, Dutton! Pick up your things and be out of your office by noon!"

"You'd better think about this, DeSoto. If you fire me, I'll go public with what I know about the Vikings and about your efforts at a cover-up."

"Get out of my sight!"

"If you need me, I'll be in my office."

"You don't have an office, Dutton! I mean it! You're fired."

"I've scheduled a news conference at 2 P.M. Would you like me to announce then that I've been fired? I'm sure they'll have plenty of questions. You know what? Why don't you come? After I've made my statement, you could field the questions about why I've been fired."

As Dutton left, DeSoto stood at the door and swore at him.

Fifteen minutes later, DeSoto phoned back. "I shouldn't have said you were fired," he said in a monotone voice. "So . . . I apologize."

"Okay."

"But you are going to be off the job for a while. You know the policy. After a shooting, you have to go on paid administrative leave until an investigation is completed."

"I know."

There was a prolonged silence.

"You're not going to say anything about the Vikings in your news conference, are you?" DeSoto asked.

"No, of course not."

"Good. Well, that's all I have to say."

"Good-bye." Dutton hung up the phone and put his elbows on the desk, cradling his head with his hands. He had a killer headache.

A few minutes later he sat up and looked around his office. *I would miss this job,* he thought. *It doesn't happen often that you can make a difference. I've made a difference here. More than two thousand arrests of career criminals without a single shot being fired, either by my officers or by the suspects we arrested. That's got to be worth something.*

In preparation for the news conference, Dutton wrote up a statement about the Monkey Boys and their activities, the attempt to arrest them, and the events leading to their deaths. He tried to word the shooting deaths of three of the gang in such a way as not to put the bungled arrest attempt in a bad light. He also planned to describe how he had been forced to shoot Chad, explaining that he had no choice once fired upon.

He dreaded the news conference but knew it was his best chance to get the media to cover it in one day and then move on to other news.

At first the news conference seemed to be going well. He had anticipated most of the questions and was able to provide clear, concise answers that seemed to satisfy most reporters.

Near the end of the conference, though, a man in the back of the room stood up. Dutton should have recognized him but didn't.

"Yes, do you have a question?"

"Chad Nieteri was my son, and I want to know why you didn't use your famous containment tactic to bring him in alive instead of killing him before he ever had a chance to explain. Everyone knows about you, Dutton. You're the one who tells his men that firing a weapon is a last resort. Why don't you practice what you preach?"

"As I said previously, when I arrived, Chad Nieteri was about to throw that young woman off a cliff. I ordered him to lay down his gun and back away. He put the gun down, and then turned and attempted to push her off the cliff. He then grabbed his gun and shot at me. At that point, I felt I had no choice but to return his fire. I did shoot him and he fell off the cliff. By the time I was able to get to him, he was already dead."

"How do we know for sure that's what happened?" Chad's dad asked. "How do we know you're not just covering up your big mistake?"

Dutton paused, remembering his promise to Kristen that he would do his best to keep her name out of the public eye, but now it looked as though he had no choice. "Kristen Boone can corroborate my story. She was there. She can tell you that what I have said is true."

Chad's dad continued. "Where is this Kristen Boone you keep talking about? I want to hear from her what really happened, and until I do, I'm not buying any of this. Chad has always been a good boy. The way I see it, you're a cowardly killer."

The next question, from a reporter, was predictable. "Where is Kristen Boone, and why haven't we heard from her?"

"She's in Idaho."

"Will you be bringing her in?"

"She is not a person of interest to us."

"Won't you need her for questioning? Has a gag order been issued? When will she be available to the media?"

"I'm not a publicist. I'm a cop. I solve crimes. My job is not to feed media frenzy. Now if you'll excuse me, I have work to do."

"Why won't you let us talk to Kristen Boone?" Chad's dad called out. "What are you hiding?"

Half an hour later, Dutton left the building. He ended up on the Angeles Crest Highway. He drove to an old cemetery. A minute later he was wandering around the grounds. He came across a headstone that had been neglected. He knelt down and absently began to pull up some of the grass that had grown around the headstone. In many respects that afternoon, he envied the man lying six feet under the ground.

Monday, May 5

After being hounded relentlessly by the media, Kristen reluctantly agreed to a news conference. A local TV station arranged for it to be held in a hotel conference room across the Snake River and not far from the Idaho Falls Temple.

The local stations were present, as well as many media representatives from Los Angeles.

In her statement, she tried to minimize her involvement in Chad's life. She did, however, talk about how she had fully cooperated with law enforcement by making Chad's laptop available to them.

"The police were able to retrieve all of the files on the laptop, and that information is what eventually led to the warrant for his arrest."

After reading her statement, she opened up the news conference for questions.

"Did you ever go with the Monkey Boys when they did a job?" one reporter asked.

"No. As I have said, I didn't know anything about that part of Chad's life."

"You must have had some knowledge of what was going on. People have been comparing you to Bonnie and Clyde."

"That is not true. We were just friends. I have nothing more to say then. Thank you and good-bye."

"Just one more question. Where are you keeping the money Chad gave you? And is it true, as some tabloids have reported, that you had an abortion last month?"

"Didn't you hear anything I said? Why won't you people believe me? I'm telling the truth!" She walked out of the conference room.

A local reporter caught up with her. "You need to go back in there."

"Why? Nobody believes me."

"If you leave now, they'll hound you. You have to stay until they're tired of you. And then they'll leave you alone."

She looked at him. He seemed to be somebody she could trust.

She returned to the news conference. "Any other questions?"

After an hour, they got tired of hearing her deny any involvement in the gang and repeatedly insist she and Chad were only friends. One by one they packed up and left until she was the only one there, except for the reporter who had urged her to stay.

"You okay?" he asked.

"I guess so."

"You did a good job. Think of today as a feeding frenzy. When it's over, the sharks leave. I'm glad you hung in there." He slung a battery pack over his shoulder. "If it's any consolation, I believe you. Can I buy you a drink?"

"I don't drink."

He smiled. "You might want to reconsider that. Sometimes getting drunk is a good thing. It's gotten me through an ugly divorce."

She shook her head sadly. "Thanks, but I don't think so."

As she stepped out of the conference room, she noticed David Carpenter standing off to the side of the lobby.

He smiled and sauntered over to her.

"That was pretty rough in there, huh?" he said. "But you did a good job. I was proud of you."

She sighed and her shoulders slumped. "Thanks, but it didn't feel like a good job. I'm just glad it's over." She looked up at him. "What brings you here?"

"I heard about the news conference and thought you might need a friend. That's all."

She smiled tiredly. "Well, you're right about that. Thanks."

David cleared his throat. "You doing anything now?"

"Why?"

"Follow me back as far as Rexburg. I want to show you something on campus."

"What do you want to show me?"

"Something I think you'll be interested in."

Forty-five minutes later she parked her car on the BYU–Idaho campus. David pulled his pickup truck in next to her.

They both got out and met on the sidewalk. "Let's go," he said.

"Where?"

"Just follow me. I want to show you something."

Because her name had been on all the news networks, she didn't feel very comfortable out in public where someone might recognize her.

He gave her a tour of every building on campus. Every time he met someone he knew, he quickly introduced her.

Nobody seemed to recognize her.

"That's about it except for the livestock building outside town," he said.

"Why the campus tour, David? I've been here before."

"That's not what I wanted to show you."

"What did you want to show me?"

"I wanted you to see that nobody here knows or cares about what the news channels are saying about you."

He stepped in front of her, looked into her eyes, and said, "What they're saying about you isn't true. Is it?"

"No."

"I didn't think so. It must be hard to be so . . . well, visible."

"It is. It makes me want to go in my room and never come out."

"I've been thinking about it. And I have an idea. But I need you to come with me to my family home evening group tonight."

She shook her head. "I have to go home."

"No, you don't. Not really. You're just embarrassed, but don't be. I'm on your side. Call your folks and tell them you're with me today. Come to the rest of my classes, and then we'll grab something to eat and then go to family home evening."

"Aren't you afraid of being seen with me?"

He laughed. "Are you kidding? I've always liked being seen with you."

She enjoyed her day with David. As before, when he introduced her in his classes, nobody made any big deal of what she had been going through.

The guys in David's apartment met with a girls' apartment for family home evening. He made a point of introducing her to everyone. His family home evening sisters, as he called them, were friendly and cute, although she wondered if some of them weren't jealous of the attention David was paying her.

At eight-thirty, when his roommates left, he told them he would be staying a little longer. He took Kristen's hand and led her outside.

"These girls have a vacancy in their apartment," he said. "What would you think about moving in with them? I already talked to them about it."

"I'm not in school."

He shrugged. "Take an online class."

"Why? It doesn't make sense for me to move here when I can live for free at home," she said.

"This place is a refuge from the storm. The way I look at it, that's what you need right now."

"You know what people are saying about me."

"Sure. But none of it is true. So what's the big deal?"

"It's been awful, David. They're saying I was part of the Monkey Boys gang and that Chad and I were . . ." She paused. "This is really embarrassing. That we were . . ."

"I know what you mean."

She took a deep breath and spoke fast. "When I found out you were at the press conference, I was so embarrassed. It kills me to know that people I grew up with are being told that Chad Nieteri and I were outlaw lovers. They kept comparing us to Bonnie and Clyde. You know what? I didn't even know who Bonnie and Clyde were." She paused. "But I do now. Chad and I weren't anything like that."

"I believe you. I came because I want to help you. Also, to see if I could talk you into moving in with my family home evening sisters. So what do you think about that?"

She thought about it. *To be able to live her life without people hounding her seemed very inviting.*

"Why go to so much trouble for me?"

He shrugged. "Because Zach is my best friend. He'd want me to take good care of his little sister."

For the next hour, for each objection she had about moving in with his family home evening sisters, he had an answer.

"Just try it for a week and see what you think," he said.

"All right, but don't be surprised if I go home in a day or two."

"Nah. With all the fun you'll be having with me, I don't think you will."

His comment made her mad, and she called him on it, but privately she could see that he might be right.

CHAPTER TWELVE

The shooting review board cleared Dutton of any possible wrong-doing in the death of Chad Nieteri, and on Thursday, May 8, Dutton was back at work in his office when DeSoto came to talk to him.

"What can I do for you?" Dutton asked.

"How long until you retire?"

"Ten years, I guess. Why do you ask?"

"There's a new program we've just instituted for those working in high-stress jobs, like yours for instance. Under the guidelines, you'd only have to work for two more years, and then you could retire with full benefits."

"Right now that sounds very tempting," Dutton said. "What's the catch?"

"We realize how difficult it is to be in the job you're in now, so we'd like to move you to headquarters where your leadership and experience could make a real difference."

"What would I be doing?"

"We'd like you to be in charge of public relations for the next two years."

Dutton shook his head in disgust, finally seeing where this was going.

"Public relations is really the heart and soul of what we do, isn't it?" Dutton said cynically.

"It is important, Dutton."

"Two years, huh? That's about how long the Sanchez lawsuit will be pending, isn't it?"

"I suppose so."

"So let me see if I understand what the job entails. You'd like me to make sure that any information about the sheriff's department is positive, right? Rather than, say, truthful."

"Two years, Dutton. It's a nine-to-five job. And then you can retire."

"I'd rather stay here."

DeSoto shook his head. "Actually, that might not be an option."

"I guess we'll see, won't we? Now if you'll excuse me, I have work to do."

Monday, May 12

On his way home from work, Dutton noticed the steering in his car seemed different. He stopped at a service station and asked them to check it out.

"Did you just get new tires?" the mechanic asked a minute later.

"No, why?"

"Well, all the lug nuts on the front tires have been loosened. You're lucky the wheels didn't fall off. I went ahead and tightened them for you."

Dutton suspected that whoever had tampered with his car had done it as a warning. *They're not going to scare me off*, he thought.

Wednesday, May 14

Dutton was home watching the kids while Laura was at the grocery store. When she came into the house, she said, "My front tire seems a little low."

He went out to the driveway and inspected the tire. Someone had punctured it in the sidewall. This didn't look like the work of some punk kid getting a thrill by an act of vandalism. Whoever had done this knew what he was doing. The puncture was small enough to cause a slow leak, and only one tire was punctured. Vandals normally slash more than one tire, and the tire loses all its pressure immediately.

Dutton imagined what might have happened. Laura would load her groceries into her car and begin to drive home. In a short time, she would realize something was wrong and pull over and stop. A car could slow down as if the driver were going to help. A single bullet was all they would need.

This was no longer a game. Someone had intended to either kill Laura or traumatize her for life.

"I need everyone in the kitchen right now!" Dutton barked.

While they gathered, he turned off the lights in the living room and looked out the window. He didn't see anyone.

Dutton joined his family in the kitchen. "All right, everyone get packed, because we're going away for a few days!"

"What?" Abigail asked.

"Where are we going?" Adam asked

"Five minutes! Get going! We'll talk about it later."

Ten minutes later they were on the road.

"The children and I need to have some kind of explanation," Laura said.

"There are some officers in the sheriff's department who are doing bad things. I found out about it, and I filed a complaint. They're not very happy with me. Tonight they tried to hurt your mom. So we're going away for a few days until things cool down."

"How long will that be?" Abigail asked.

"I'm not sure."

"This isn't fair," she complained.

"I know," he said.

He drove north on Highway 101, up the California coast, constantly watching his rearview mirror to determine if anyone was following them. Laura and the kids eventually fell asleep, and he drove until three in the morning before stopping at a motel to sleep.

Thursday, May 15

Dutton and his family slept until nine, got cleaned up, then had breakfast. After breakfast they continued north.

They stopped for the night at a motel in Coos Bay, Oregon. That afternoon they all took a walk on the beach and then visited a botanical garden. Its beauty was mostly lost on Dutton. He was too consumed with his own problems and worried about the safety of his family.

Friday, May 16

Early the next morning, while the kids were still asleep, Dutton and Laura walked along the beach.

"How bad is it?" she asked.

"It's pretty bad. It's not just one person out to get me."

"How many are there?" she asked.

"I'm not sure. Somewhere between fifteen and twenty. The problem is I don't know who they are, so it could be anyone. And what's worse is that nobody at headquarters is going to help me."

"Why won't they help you?"

"They're facing a huge lawsuit plus the possibility of having the entire sheriff's department put under federal direction. Nobody wants that."

"It will blow over."

"Even if a few rogue cops go to jail, some will avoid being found out. There's never going to be a time when I'll feel that you and the kids are safe. I don't know what to do, Laura."

"You'll do what's right."

"What's right for you and the kids or what's right for my career or what's right for NORSAT?" he asked.

"I don't know what to tell you."

He reached for her hand. "Can I tell you something? I love my job. When I look back and see the improvements we've made, I get a real feeling of satisfaction."

"And you should. You've saved people's lives."

He put his arm around her. "Maybe now is the time to get out, not only to save me but to save you and the kids."

"What do you mean?"

"I've thought a lot about it. The way I see it, there's no choice. I have to quit my job and then we have to move far away."

"But your job is your life."

"It's not my life. You and the kids are my life."

"But to quit your job after all you've done. There must be another solution."

"I don't think so. Quitting is what's best for us, and that's what I'm going to do."

Dutton and Laura told their children after breakfast, then rented an RV and headed south, back to L.A. On the way, he called DeSoto and told him he was quitting.

"Are you sure?" DeSoto asked.

"I'm sure."

"It's probably for the best. I'll start the paperwork."

After finishing with DeSoto, he turned to Laura. "So much for thinking I was irreplaceable."

"You are irreplaceable. They just don't know it yet."

And then he called Delilah.

"Where have you been?" she asked. "Everyone's been asking about you."

"I'm sure they have. Look, I'm quitting my job and moving out of state. I want to come back to pick up some things at the house. When we do that, I want our route and the neighborhood secured."

"What are you talking about, Chief? You can't quit. Who would I harass?"

"Listen to me, Delilah, my family and I are targets. We're coming in to pick up a few things. I'll have the rest moved. I want the area secured."

"When are you going to be here?" Delilah asked.

"When could you be ready for us?"

"Give me a couple of hours."

*　　　*　　　*

At that same moment, Kristen and David were hiking in the Grand Teton National Forest. When they first started they had talked a lot, but now that the trail was getting steeper, they didn't say much, partly out of admiration for the beauty around them, and partly to conserve energy.

After about an hour, they took a break, and Kristen pulled out a crumpled and food-stained envelope from her backpack.

"What's that?"

"It's the letter you sent me on your mission. I know I never wrote you back. When it came, I was going through a rough time, so it made me mad. I threw it in the kitchen garbage."

He smiled. "My English teachers used to do that too."

"A couple of days later I felt bad and dug it out. By then it was covered with dirt and food. But I kept it anyway. I'll always keep it. I think you were inspired to write it."

"Maybe so. The idea came out of nowhere, and it wouldn't go away. Do you ever have things like that happen to you?"

She remembered the warning she'd felt not be alone with Chad in his apartment but was too embarrassed to tell David about it, so she simply said, "Sometimes."

An hour later, though, a thought did come into her mind. *I need to call Dutton.* At first she tried to talk herself out of it. *It makes no sense for me to call Dutton. What would I say? He's so busy. It makes no sense to call him.*

The thought went away for a while, but a few minutes later, it came back again, even stronger.

She stopped walking.

"Something wrong?" David asked.

"I need to call Dutton."

"Who's Dutton?"

"He's the police officer who saved my life," she said. "He lives in Los Angeles."

"Why do you need to call him?"

"I don't know. I just do."

"Do you have your cell phone?" he asked.

"No, I left it in your truck."

"I didn't bring mine either."

"We'll have to go back then," she said.

"Why?"

"I made a promise to myself that from now on I'll listen to the promptings I receive."

He nodded. "Let's go then."

"Thank you, David."

*   *   *

Dutton and his family drove slowly into their neighborhood. Overhead a helicopter hovered in place. The streets were blocked by police cars with flashing lights.

Delilah met them in the front yard. "We're ready for you, Chief. Just so you know, we've got more security here than we'd have for the president. Oh, by the way, if you go out to the garden, don't pick any vegetables or you might be looking into the barrel of an automatic weapon."

He laughed. "Thanks for the warning." He turned to his family. "Let's try not to take too long."

"You do some packing, too," Delilah said. "I'll stay out here."

He grabbed a few clothes but spent most of his time gathering file folders and putting them in boxes. He could not leave behind his copies of files or his computer. He didn't want any reports about the Vikings to conveniently get lost.

Adam and Gabe were too young to know what was happening, but twelve-year-old Abigail was crying. "I don't want to move!"

"I know, Baby. Me either, but it's what we have to do."

An hour later they were ready to go. He gave the house key to

Delilah. "As soon as we know where we're going to live, I'll let you know, so you can open the place up for the movers."

"I'll do that."

Dutton could see his family was waiting for him in the RV.

"Well, I'd better get going. Thanks for all your help," he said.

Delilah looked at him. Tears were glistening in her eyes. It was awkward for both of them. Finally she smiled and said, "Dutton, I swear, if you try to salute me, I'll wring your neck."

They gave each other a hug. "It's been a singular pleasure to serve with you, sir," she said.

"The pleasure has been mine."

"Okay, your wife is looking a little worried, so get out of here," she said.

As they were pulling out of the driveway, Delilah raised her hand.

From bushes and behind garbage cans SWAT team members stood to attention and saluted as they drove by.

The helicopter followed them for an hour, and then it flew in front of them, dipped down as if to say good-bye, and flew away.

Half an hour later, Dutton's cell phone rang.

"Dutton, here," he said.

"Uh, so, uh, how's it going?" Kristen stammered.

"Hi, Kristen. Everything's fine. How are things going with you?"

"Okay. Better. I'm sorry. I won't keep you. I don't even know why I called. I just had a feeling that I should. I don't know why." She hesitated. "Do you?"

Dutton didn't like to be dependent on anyone, and maybe if it was just him he wouldn't have said anything, but he had a family to take care of. "Actually, I think I might know. I just quit my job, and, well, I've been thinking about the offer your dad made, about your grandparents' place being available. Do you think that's still a possibility? At least for a little while?"

"Of course. It would be perfect. They're still on their mission, and the house is just empty."

"Are you sure it would be okay with your folks?"

"Yeah, sure, they'd love to have you. Give them a call if you want. I'll give you their number."

Tuesday, May 20

Dutton and his family pulled up to Kristen's grandparents' place at three in the afternoon. Kristen, her folks, and David came out of the house to welcome them.

Dutton introduced his family to the others and Kristen introduced David to the Duttons, then Kristen's mom put her hand on Laura's arm and said, "We'll be grateful forever for what your husband did to save Kristen. We're so glad you're going to stay here."

"Thank you. It's so beautiful," Laura said. "Just one question, though. Where's the closest mall?"

Everyone except Laura laughed.

An hour later David and Kristen said good-bye to everyone and drove away.

"Could you pull over?" Kristen asked a few minutes later.

"Okay." After stopping, David could see Kristen was trembling. "What's wrong?"

"Over there in the trees is where Chad almost killed me."

"Oh."

She sighed. "I haven't been there since then, but I still have nightmares. When my grandparents get back from their mission, I don't want to be afraid of driving past here to visit them. Will you come with me to where it happened?"

"If you want me to."

She led him across the pasture, through the woods, and to the cliff. They sat in the shade while she described what had happened there, how Chad had threatened to push her off the cliff and how Dutton had finally had to shoot Chad.

"He fell off here and landed below. It was awful."

"Of course it was," he said.

She shook her head. "You don't know what Chad was like. When he got mad, he was vicious." She turned to him. "This is kind of weird to ask, but will you go with me to the bottom of the cliff? I want to see where Chad's body landed when he fell."

A few minutes later they reached the bottom of the cliff. She looked up to where they had been standing, then pointed to the ground a few steps away. "It was just over there somewhere."

They found a place where the weeds were matted down.

"This must be where he died," she said, staring at the spot. "I'm glad I saw it. Maybe it will help the nightmares to go away. I would love to get a good night's sleep again."

"I'm sorry you had to go through this," he said.

She shook her head. "That's just it. If I'd made better choices early on, then none of it would have ever happened." With tears in her eyes, she added, "I'm so disappointed in myself. Sometimes I feel that I don't deserve to ever be happy again."

"Are you ever going to repeat the mistakes you made?" he asked.

"No, never."

"Then maybe you should just trust in the Savior and move on with your life."

"That's easy for you to say. You've never made any serious mistakes."

"I've spent the past two years watching what the Atonement can do for those who repent. Sometimes I feel like I've lived a hundred years through their experiences. The Atonement worked for all of them. I'm sure it will work for you too."

"Maybe someday Father in Heaven will forgive me. I'm just not sure I'll ever be able to forgive myself."

"You'll have to sooner or later, won't you?"

She sighed. "I suppose so." She turned and gave him a hug. "Thanks for coming here with me, and thanks for being such a big help to me. I feel a lot better now. Let's go."

They ended up at David's house with his family. His folks asked how her brother Zach was doing on his mission. She told them a few things but was surprised when they didn't ask more questions about him. Always before, her only function in David's family was to provide news of Zach. She wondered how that had changed.

"Stay for dinner, and I'll cook you the best Dutch-oven meal you've ever had," David said.

She agreed to stay but had no idea it would take so long. They didn't eat until ten-thirty that night.

"So, what do you think?" he asked as she dug into a plate of potatoes cooked up with large quantities of crisp bacon, cheese, onions, and the secret ingredient, 7-Up.

"I can't tell. I'm so starved I'm not taking the time to taste it," she joked.

He smiled. "Sorry. I didn't think it would take this long. This is only the second time I've done this."

"It was worth the wait. This is so good."

After they finished eating, she helped him clean up, then he took her home. They parked in the driveway in front of her house and talked. "This has been fun. I had a really good time," she said.

"My pleasure."

"I'll give Zach a good report on you when he gets back," she said.

"You think I'm doing this only because you're his sister?" he asked.

"I don't know. Why are you spending time with me?"

"I'll tell you sometime," he said.

They talked for another hour.

"Can I tell you something?" she asked. "I've gone through some really hard times over these past few months. I've been so scared that I have had a hard time sleeping. Then, during the day, I've been nervous and upset, worrying about Chad and his threats, and since he died, about all the news people. But I feel really calm when I'm with you."

"I'm glad. If you're having a bad night and you can't sleep, call me and we'll talk." He smiled. "Besides, I'm kind of boring, so I'll probably put you to sleep right away."

"You, boring? Not to me."

"Thanks. I'm serious, though, call me if you can't sleep."

They sat without speaking for a few minutes, and David reached to take hold of her hand. She let him take it.

Kristen said, "Do you remember that one dance we were at where the older girls were being rude, and you ignored them and danced with me? I thought that was really cool."

"We go back a long way," he said. "You used to be just Zach's little sister, but you've grown up."

When he finally took her to the door, he kissed her for the first time. It was a very proper kiss, not anything like those she had shared with Chad. But it was still a thrill.

That night she didn't have any nightmares.

*   *   *

Kristen spent the rest of the summer on the campus of BYU–Idaho. During the day she worked on two online classes. Almost every evening she spent time with David.

After a couple of weeks on campus, they went to the temple to do baptisms for the dead.

By the time Kristen had changed into street clothes and tried to do something with her hair, she found David at the baptismal area desk talking to Brother and Sister Meyers, two of the temple officiators. She caught them in the middle of their conversation.

"So how many grandchildren do you have?" David asked.

"Fifteen."

David broke into a big grin. "Wow, fifteen? Tell me about them."

"Our grandson Alex graduated with honors from BYU. And now he's in law school at Columbia University," Brother Meyers said.

"Hey, even to get into Columbia is impressive. You must be really proud of him!" David said.

David is the nicest guy I've ever known, Kristen thought. *He always tries to make people feel good about themselves. Nothing like Chad. He only cared about himself.*

She told David she'd forgotten something in the dressing room. On her way there, she stopped in the hall to offer a silent prayer. *Father in Heaven, I thank thee for being so kind to me. I thank thee for the Savior's atonement. I thank thee that it's okay for me to be here in thy temple. I thank thee for giving me a friend like David. In the name of Jesus Christ, amen.*

When she rejoined David, she tried to be as good a listener as he was as Brother and Sister Meyers continued to boast about their family.

When a youth group from another ward arrived to do baptisms, Brother and Sister Meyers excused themselves. David casually put his arm around Kristen, and sang a line from an old country-western song, "'Hey, Good-Lookin', what you got cookin'? How's about cookin' something up with me?'"

"David, please, we're in the temple," she teased.

"What are you saying? You don't like my singing?" he asked with a grin.

"I'm not exactly saying that. I'm just saying that—"

He pouted, "Gee, I've worked so hard on it."

She laughed. "Well, keep working."

He gave her a hug. "What do you say we go get something to eat. My treat."

As they went through the temple cafeteria line, David asked her, "What kind of pie are you going to get?"

"I can't decide. Either chocolate cream or apple."

"That's easy." He grabbed a piece of each and put them on their tray.

"I don't need two pieces of pie," she said.

"Take a taste of both. Whichever one you want, I'll take the other."

"David, you've got to quit spoiling me."

"It's just pie, Kristen. Besides, I like to spoil you a little."

As they ate and talked, it seemed to Kristen that the whole room was full of light. She felt peace of mind and hope for the future.

"What do you see yourself doing in five years?" she asked.

"I've thought a lot about that. My dad has always wanted me to take over the farm, and for a long time it wasn't something I wanted to do. But lately I've changed my mind. Dad's always worked hard, but there are new technologies—better ways to run the farm, more like a business. Living on a farm was a good way to grow up. I'm thinking I'd like to give my kids the same advantages. How about you? Are you going to go back to California for school?"

"No, my traveling days are over. I'm going to finish up at BYU–Idaho."

He grinned at her.

"What?" she asked.

"Nothing. I'm just glad to hear that."

Later, as they were leaving the temple, they stopped to watch as a photographer was taking pictures of a bridal party.

"David, you want to know how I feel when I'm with you?"

"Tell me."

She sighed. "I feel like I've come home."

"I feel the same way," he said.

The photographer had finished with the bride and groom and was now taking pictures of the bride by herself.

"You want to do that sometime?" David asked.

"Yeah, sometime, if I meet the right guy."

He reached for her hand. "I mean with me."

She was shocked and turned to look at him. "Are you teasing?"

"No, I'm serious. You know what? When we were in the temple cafeteria, I felt like we were already married."

He wasn't grinning, like he should have been if he was just kidding. She gave him a long look, then finally said, "Do you really think we should get married?"

He studied her face. "Sure, why not? We get along pretty good, don't we?"

"David, this is crazy. You don't really know anything about me."

"What do you mean? I've known you since you were a little girl. I know your family. Heck, your brother is my best friend."

"Well, we do get along great. You're the nicest guy I've ever known. And whenever I've thought about getting married, I've always pictured someone like you. But . . ."

"Then this is your lucky day, because it turns out I'm available."

"I don't know what to say."

"I know you have trouble sleeping at night. If I were with you at night, then you'd feel safe."

She blushed.

"What do you think?" he urged.

"Well, there's nobody I would rather have next to me in bed—" She caught herself. "Oh, that didn't come out right. I mean—"

David was grinning at her.

"So, you'll give it some thought?" he asked.

A short time later David took her back to her apartment. He had a test the next day and couldn't stay, so he gave her a quick hug and then said good night.

She slept soundly until a little before seven the next morning. By the time she woke up, whatever magic had existed between them at the temple was now gone. She opened her eyes, blinked, sat straight up in bed, and said to herself, "Oh, my gosh, what have I done?"

She hurriedly pulled on a pair of jeans and a sweatshirt, but kept her slippers on, then drove to David's apartment. She banged on the door until his roommate came to the door in pajamas.

"I need to talk to David!"

"He went running. He's probably over at the track."

"So, are you going to sleep all day?" Kristen called back to him as she headed for the track.

David was surprised to see her. "Good morning, you want to run?"

It was hard to keep up with him in her slippers. "We need to talk. I'm so sorry about yesterday. I don't know what I was thinking. Forget what I said about us getting married. I think it was because we spent so much time in the temple. Let's promise ourselves never to go there together again."

"I don't suppose you could pick up the pace any, right?" he asked with a grin.

"I'm in my slippers, for crying out loud!"

"Sorry." He slowed to a walk. "So you're having second thoughts, huh?"

"*Second* thoughts?" she asked. "No, third, fourth, tenth thoughts. We're not good candidates for marriage. It only seems that way because I'm really needy, and you're a Boy Scout, always trying to do a good deed. If I were a lost cocker spaniel, you would take me in, feed me, and put a big bowl of water in the kitchen for me. That's the kind of person you are."

He stopped walking and turned to look at her with a hurt expression. "Am I supposed to be understanding any of this?"

They stood facing each other. "Don't you see?" she asked. "If we did get married, then in a couple of years you'd realize you only married me because I was having a hard time and you wanted to help out. That's not a good reason to get married."

"I'm pretty sure I love you, Kristen."

"You do? Why?"

"I'm always happy when I'm with you. Isn't that worth something?"

"Wait a minute. I'm not finished. I can't believe I said I wanted to wake up with you in bed. I didn't mean—"

"I know what you didn't mean," he said.

"What I meant was—"

"I know what you meant. And I feel the same way."

"I'm so sorry, David. I can't marry you. I'm not sure I can marry anyone. It's such a big decision. I don't know how anyone makes a decision that lasts forever. That's all I have to say. I've got to go."

He reached out to take her hand, but she backed away from him.

"No, go exercise," she called out to him. "I'm going back to bed."

All that day she was tortured by her thoughts. *I'm not worthy of*

David. He's always been so good, and the way I behaved in California revealed how weak and shallow I am. It's just so hard because I've always liked David. I wish he would just leave me alone. She paused. *No, that's not what I want either. Oh, I'm not sure what I want.*

He tried to call her that night, but she didn't pick up. Finally, just before curfew, he dropped by her apartment. "I can't stay long. There's a dance Friday night. Would you go with me?" he asked.

"I'm not sure. Let me think about it."

"It's just a dance, Kristen, okay? That's all it is. I know you like to dance."

"All right, all right," she said irritably. "I'll go with you."

In her mind she pictured herself as being aloof at the dance, but on Friday night, once she began to dance, all those plans went out the window. "This is so fun!" she called out to him after they had been dancing for an hour.

"You want to take a break?" he asked, almost pleading.

"No, I'm fine! I love dancing . . ." As an afterthought, she added, "With you."

Forty-five minutes later she finally agreed to sit down and have something to drink. That lasted ten minutes, and then she dragged him back onto the floor. He went reluctantly, stretching his aching back.

Even though most people had already gone, they danced to the very end.

"You want to drop me off at the hospital?" he asked as they left the building. "I'm sure a little reconstructive surgery on my feet will have me up and around in no time."

"You are such a whiner," she teased.

They started walking toward her apartment.

"I was thinking about what I asked you at the temple, you know, about us getting married," he said. "You were right. I shouldn't have brought it up."

She felt depressed but didn't want him to know it. "I'm glad you agree."

"Trying to decide to get married can be very difficult. Let me ask you a few other questions that aren't as earth-shattering. How would you feel if we went dancing every weekend for the rest of the summer?"

"I would like that very much."

"What if we keep dancing during fall semester?" he asked.

"That'd be good, too."

"What if we go to a dance every weekend for the rest of our lives?" he asked.

"I never get tired of dancing."

"Really? We get along well too, don't we? What if we agreed to talk to each other every day? You could tell me how your day went, and I would do the same for you."

She nodded. "I like talking to you."

"What if we ate all our meals together?" he asked. "That way we could talk and get something to eat at the same time."

She knew where this was heading, but all of a sudden she wasn't sure she wanted to stop it. "Sure. I love hanging out with you."

"What if we started going together to the temple once or twice a month?" he asked.

"I can see that would be a good thing to do."

"What if, at the close of every day, we had prayer together?" he asked.

"I'd like that."

"And every morning we woke up next to each other. How would you feel about that?"

She couldn't look him in the eye, but, with her gaze fixed on the ground, she said softly, "I like that idea too."

"Well, you know what? We can do all of those things, but there's just one catch."

"What?" she asked.

"We'll have to get married."

She let out a huge sigh. "I suppose you're right."

"You don't seem too excited about the idea," he said.

"Are you sure you want to do this? There will always be people who remember what cable news channels have said about me."

"Was any of it true?"

"I didn't even know Chad and his friends were criminals."

"No. Of course you didn't."

"How much do you want to know about Chad and me?"

"Are you worthy of a temple recommend?"

"Yes, I am."

"That's all I need to know. I love you, Kristen. Let's get married."

"What about Zach? You think he'll be mad at me for taking you away from him? I mean, you were his best friend."

"We'll still be friends. I'll go hunting and fishing with him."

She nodded. "He'll like that."

"How do you feel about me?" he asked.

"I've always loved you, even when I was little, but now, even more, and in a different way."

That was his cue. He stopped walking and turned Kristen toward him. Then he kissed her.

After he kissed her, he said, "Well, what do you think? That wasn't so bad, was it?"

"No, not bad at all," she smiled.

"That's something else we can do every day, after we're married. So what do you say?"

"You're very persuasive, Mr. Carpenter," she said.

Both of them broke into silly grins.

*   *   *

Kristen and David were married in December, after Zach returned home from his mission.

Dutton and Laura attended the wedding. They were now living in Rexburg where Dutton was working as a substitute school teacher.

Dutton had liked David from the moment he met him. *He's a nice kid,* Dutton thought as David and Kristen were kneeling across from each other in the temple. *I hope they're as happy as Laura and I are.*

He smiled as he thought about all that had happened to him. *It was hard, but it's over now.*

*   *   *

Much later that night, David stood up as Kristen came out of the bathroom into the bedroom of their bridal suite.

"You promised we'd dance every night," she said.

He seemed a little confused. "I did?"

"You did."

He nodded. "We'll dance then."

He surfed the cable channels until he found something they could dance to.

After a few minutes of dancing, she said, "That will fulfill that requirement."

"Anything else?" he asked.

"You also said we'd pray every night."

They knelt by the side of the bed and had their first family prayer. As they got up from their knees, David asked, "Did I promise anything else?"

"Not as I recall." She yawned and stretched. "Well, good night, David. Don't let the bedbugs bite." She got into bed, turned on her side, facing away from him, and closed her eyes.

David gently lobbed a pillow at her.

She sat up with a scowl on her face. "So that's the way it's going to be, is it?" She grabbed two pillows and tossed one after another at him.

But their pillow fight didn't last very long.